THE LAST TRUMPET

Dr. Bruce E. Powell

THE LAST TRUMPET

Dr. Bruce E. Powell

Sterling House Publisher
Pittsburgh, PA

Sterling House Mass Market Paperback
ISBN 1-156315-049-2

© Copyright 1998 Dr. Bruce Powell
All rights reserved
First Printing—1998

Request for information should be addressed to:

Sterling House Publisher
The Sterling Building
440 Friday Road
Department T-101
Pittsburgh, PA 15209

Cover design & Typesetting: Drawing Board Studios

Printed in the United States of America

THE RAPTURE

1

The Pope turned and said, "Cardinal Miles, would you please take these papers into your office and go over them." Miles took the papers and started into his office. As he approached the door he heard a sound, like something hitting the floor. He turned and the Pope was gone, but his clothes were laying on the floor! Miles stood there stunned, what on earth could have happened, he thought. They were there together just a moment ago and now the Pope was gone. Miles had a weird feeling, he had heard of the Rapture, even though the word rapture per sey, was not found in his Bible. He had heard people speak about it, but really had never given it too much thought. To him it simply seemed incredible that the God he served would be so cruel, as to take out all the loved ones, all little babies and young children and leave others to grieve. No, this had to be something else, this must be some kind of intervention from a relm we really don't understand, he thought.

Miles did not panic, he calmly walked into his own office, which was connected to the Pope's by a door. He turned on his television set and a very worried, trembling, stuttering commentator was trying to talk, "Fo . . . Fol . . . Folks, I . . . I . . . I . . . don . . . don't know wha . . . what has ha . . . ha . . . pened, but . . . but the reports we . . . wee . . . we are getting; sa . . . say . . . people everywhere have dis . . . disap . . . peared. We . .

1

. wee . . . we're trying to rea . . . reach th . . . the Pope, ma . . . may . . . maybe . . . he will ha . . . have some answers. The guy was as white as a sheet, his knees were knocking, and his jaw was jerking so hard, it was impossible for him to communicate . . . He was upset, to put it mildly.

Miles heard the phone ring in the Pope's office. He ran, picked it up and answered, "Cardinal Miles here."

A very disturbed and troubled voice on the line said, "Your Grace, we are receiving calls from all over the world. Do you know what is happening?" Miles recognized the voice, as one of the switchboard operators in the Vatican.

Miles at that point became extremely distressed and uncertain about everything, in fact he just didn't know what to think. Is this real?

"All I know, I was with the Pope one minute, I turned to go into my office and I heard a thump, I guess it was his clothes. All he had on is laying here on the floor, but our Pope is gone."

The operator was frightened; her heart was racing and she herself was somewhat in a daze as she said, "Your Grace, in these many calls that are coming in, they say, people, little babies, and small children everywhere have disappeared. Two ladies that sat beside me here have vanished. Their clothes, and all they had on are still here, but they are gone. What can we say to this? What can we do? I can't believe this, this is too much. Can the Church make a statement on this? Is there anything that can be said to explain this to people?"

Miles knew he had to face this issue; he was next in line and the Pope presumably was gone. He hesitated then said, "Yes, the Church will make a statement. Tell the callers to stay tuned to the TV. Direct the media here to the Pope's office, I'll make a statement." In his heart and mind, he was saying to himself, The U.F.O's have certainly paid us a visit. All the rumors and things that had been published and seen about U.F.O's, suddenly became a reality, and certainly it seemed as if their move on humans of earth had affected the entire world.

Miles was deeply troubled, this is just beyond the understanding of mortal man, he thought. But he knew he had to make a decision, he was the most recognized church leader in the world. He had to make a comment on this and the only thing that made sense to him, was a visit from another realm that is far more advanced. He knew whatever statement he made would influence the thinking of millions; who were looking to him for the answer. Frankly, I don't have an answer, he thought.

In a matter of minutes, a news team was ushered into the office with all their equipment, and began to set up.

A very excited commentator, who was as pale as death, said, "Father, could you give us a statement and explain what is going on? This will go out live all over the world."

By this time Miles had regained his composure somewhat. He said, "Yes, I'll make a statement."

The lights and the cameras were turned on, and the commentator said, "Folks, we are live at the Vatican, in the Pope's office. We have with us Cardinal Miles Abraham, who will make an official statement for the Church at this time . . . Father," and he made a gesture to Miles.

Miles was very calm and composed; although he, himself, did not understand this, he knew enough to know he had to go on. It was his responsibility, now the buck stopped with him. As the cameras focused upon him, Miles began, "Beloved, be calm, this phenomenal thing that has happened is something none of us can understand at this time. It is catastrophic and definitely an intervention of some kind from outer space, maybe U.F.O.'s, who knows? Nothing of this magnitude has happened before, as far as it's known by man in recorded history. But this is not the first time something similar to this has happened, only on a lesser scale. Our Bible gives us at least two accounts that I can think of, off the top of my head. Enoch, in the fifth chapter of Genesis, vanished, *for God took him*, is the only explanation given; he disappeared as seemingly so many have today."

"Then, there was Elijah, in II Kings the second chapter; he was swept away and disappeared into the heavens. It is evident to me there is another, far more advanced form of life than we are able to understand. These are things we don't, and can't know as yet, but People, life is that way. There are so many things none of us can comprehend as yet.—So what are we going to do?—Are we going to stand around wondering, looking dumbfounded?—Or are we going to get on with our lives? I believe we should get on with the business of living. We do not know the extent of this as yet, but stay calm, there has to be an explanation some where for everything. I'll be very frank, I don't understand this any more than any of you, but life goes on. Let's pull together and move on. Because of this, as has been the case in all great disastrous happenings, we, the people of the world will be drawn together and we will work our way through this chaotic time. Let us seize the opportunity and unite our world and move forward."

The cameras were turned off, and Miles' comments were transmitted around the world over television.

Upon further investigation Miles discovered many of the people at the Vatican had vanished, and so it was all over the earth. Many heads of State, people from all walks of life, all little babies, and all small children, all vanished, but their earthly possessions: clothes, shoes, hats, rings, watches, false teeth, glasses, hearing aids, pacemakers, artificial limbs, and such, fell and remained where they were, but their bodies seemingly vanished into thin air.

The whole world staggered in a state of shock. There was utter chaos. Planes, cars, buses and trains had gone out of control and crashed as many who were at the controls were no longer there, and many, many people died.

Simultaneous with the phenomenal disappearances, on the mountains of Israel, a great coalition army had gathered because of the trouble that had been brewing for several years in the middle East between Israel and the other nations of that region. Finally Russia along with Iran, Iraq, Turkey, Libya and Germany had decided to put a stop to the trouble once and for all. They moved against Israel in great force to crush her once and forever. The United Nations, after being disregarded on several occasion, at the same second as the mass disappearance, let go with one of it's missiles. The missile was loaded with cobalt. It destroyed all but a sixth part of that great Army in a flash. It melted the eyes out of the sockets and the flesh off the bones of the men and women of the great coalition. It was horrible, never before had a weapon such as this been unleashed against men.

Pictures of this destruction were also flashed around the world. It was something for all the world to see and to take notice of. It was awesome to realize that such a deadly weapon system existed. Miles wondered, was the phenomenal disappearance of people in some way caused by this horrible explosion?

Never in all the history of mankind had there been such an unusual awakening as to how vulnerable man really is. There was great sorrow and mourning all over the world. Many mothers, fathers and grand parents watched their little babies and small children just simply vanish out of their arms. It took time for people to settle down and realize this thing was real, but as Miles had said, life goes on.

Three days went by and Miles was on the phone most of the day and night, surveying the results within the Catholic church and receiving calls with questions from the world. He soon realized, that people were looking to him for leadership, so slowly he took charge, and everywhere he advised people to fill the voids and move forward. Most of all he advised people everywhere to pull together, and there was a spirit of cooperation every where as far as Miles new.

On the fourth day, the phone in the Pope's office rang. Miles answered, "Father Miles here."

The operator said, "Your Grace, I have a Mr. Doyle Davis from the United Nations on the line. He's asking to speak to you.

"Thank you operator, please put him through."

A very stern, yet troubled voice said, "Father, this is Doyle Davis at the United Nations. I saw you on TV, and I realize as you indicated, we must pick up the pieces and get on with our lives. You have come to the attention of all the world, with your wisdom and with your calm common sense message. Also, you are in the place of spiritual leadership unequaled in the world. We need someone of your moral stature and intelligence to guide us at this time. Would you consider coming to New York, to United Nations, and help us get things back to normal?"

Miles caught his breath; this would be his greatest opportunity to seize the power he had always wanted. "Yes, I would love to come and do what I can. Can you give me two weeks to get things back in order here?"

"Yes, as long as we know you are coming, we can plan and make the arrangements."

"I shall look forward to meeting you, Mr. Davis; I'm sure things will come together again and anew. In fact, I believe this will be a good time to bring our world together as one man. There are many new things that can be set in motion to make our world a better and safer place. I long for peace on earth and good will to all men."

"Thank you, Father, we will start the wheels turning, making ready for your visit. In fact we will do a head count and evaluate the ones left. We shall try to have representation from every nation, and also from every major religion. Will you bring representation with you from the Catholic church?"

"Yes I will, good bye for now, Mr. Davis. In the meantime, feel free to call me if I can be of help."

Miles called all the people of the Vatican together. He was amazed; they all looked to him for direction, so he took complete charge. He spent the next two weeks getting things back in order. Many key people of the church had vanished, but as it was with him, there were others who were next in line to step in and fill the vacated position. Within two weeks the hierarchy was back together, and functioning almost normally.

Miles and his staff boarded the Pope's jet for New York two weeks after he talked to Mr. Davis. The flight was one of great anticipation. The waiting world was ready for him; this would be his greatest challenge. Now he had the opportunity to set in order a proper united world. His vision was Utopia, where all would have plenty, and he would be the head over all the nations of the earth. He felt such power, such pride! He had come a long way and much had been accomplished from the day, when he, as a young Jewish boy, had met Father Kolas the Catholic Priest on the street in New York city.

As he flew, his mind went back in time. He was the son of Jewish parents in New York City. He was one of seven children in a typical Jewish neighborhood, brought up for the first thirteen years of his life in typical Jewish fashion. He was taught to observe all the rituals and ceremonies of the Jewish faith. But there was something about that religion that he could not agree with nor take to; it simply left him empty. He went to the Synagogue because he was forced to go, but his heart was never in it.

One morning when he was fourteen, as he was walking down the street leading to his house he met the local Catholic Priest, Father Kolas.

"Hello son, I'm Father Kolas, and what is your name?". The priest stopped and looked kindly and lovingly at young Miles.

Miles was not used to attention; he was next to the youngest of seven, and most of the time he was put down by his older brothers and sisters.

"Hello Father, I'm Miles Abraham", there was a feeling of excitement that passed over his young being, over the fact that someone noticed him.

"Where are you headed, Son?" asked the old priest.

"Home, but I'm bored, Father. It seems there is just nothing for young people to do around here."

"Why not come to the church with me? There are many things there I can show you. Perhaps some of them will be of interest to you."

Miles caught his breath, "Golly, I'd love to Father. You sure it will be all right, me being Jewish and all that?"

"That doesn't matter young man, come, there are

many things in life. Perhaps you will see something in the Church, a young man your age should never be bored with life."

That was the beginning of his life in the Catholic church. His folks utterly and totally rejected him, and expelled him from their home when he expressed the desire to become a Catholic priest. As a result of that rejection, Father Kolas adopted him and schooled him for the priesthood. He was well qualified and loved. Over the next forty years Miles had grown into a well developed man, both mentally and physically. He was five feet ten inches tall and weighed one hundred and seventy pounds, and remained at that weight year after year. His hair was straight, thick and black and he had brown eyes. He could not be classified as handsome, yet not homely either, but he was not a man women would go wild over, and he would not regard his desire for women. When he had evil thoughts, he could cut them off and think on other things. He was very intelligent, with a great personality and had risen through the ranks to where he was at the great disappearance of people; a Cardinal, secretary to the Pope. In his heart he was in the church because of the advantage, the greatness and the prestige. Now he was the head of the Catholic church, on his way to address the United Nations and help in the establishment of a new world order.

As the large jet circled and came in for the landing he could see on the field below a large crowd of people with the red carpet out, waiting for his arrival. He knew this would be the greatest time of his life up to this moment. He was very excited and thrilled; what a wonderful time this was!

The jet did not stop at the regular terminal, the Mayor of New York and Mr. Davis had set aside a large area on the open field for the reception. The red carpet was rolled out and up to the steps where Miles and his party touched the ground. There was a very large military band and a Marine guard with many dignitaries with all the media represented with their microphones, lights and cameras. It was quite a reception. As Miles came down the steps and approached the microphone, the Mayor and Mr. Davis were standing just behind it.

"Your Grace, welcome to New York City, I'm the mayor of this fair city", and he extended his hand.

Mr. Davis also extended his hand, "I'm Mr. Davis, welcome to United Nations, your Grace."

A marine M/Sgt. moved forward and presented Miles with a key as the Mayor said, "Your Grace, please accept this key to this city."

Miles took the key, and moved up close to the microphone stand. He spoke in a very humble tone, "Thank you, Mr Mayor. Mr. Davis and my fellow citizens. On behalf of the Catholic church I consider it a great honor to be here. I realize this is an extremely troubled time, but we can look at this time with a positive approach. It presents us with the opportunity to move our world forward as never before. There has never been a time in history since the tower of Babel when we as a world were more united. We all realize how much we need to work together. I believe with all my heart we have been invaded from outer space, therefore we must unite and work with all there is within us, to develop our selves. I am here to help in what ever way I can."

The Mayor and Mr. Davis moved around facing the cameras and the crowd, and stood beside Miles.

"Thank you for coming Your Grace", the Mayor said. "We want to make you and your party as comfortable as possible, while you are here. The city is yours and if there is anything you need, please let it be known."

Mr. Davis spoke, "On behalf of the United Nations we want to welcome you and your staff. We have called a special session of the Untied Nations on next Monday morning, and we would love for you to address the world from there at that time, Your Grace."

After all the reception speeches, rituals and ceremonies, he and his staff were taken by limousines to one of New York's finest hotels. There they were established in large plush suites.

Mr. Davis and two other officials, along with four security agents, accompanied Miles into his suite to make sure he was well satisfied with the accommodations. After they all looked the place over, and the security people had checked everything out, Mr. Davis said, "Now Father, we want you to be comfortable. Anything you need, ask for it. We have instructed the hotel, the United Nations will pick up all tabs.

Miles and his staff received royal treatment, the very best. Miles had
truly become in a little over two weeks time, A PRINCE AMONG MEN.

2

THE NEW
BEGINNING

Miles was ushered into the famous hall of United Nations with a security agent at his side, two in front and two behind. As they entered, a loud voice proclaimed, "His Grace, Cardinal Miles Abraham." The five security people escorted Miles up the main aisle. Everyone in the large assembly hall stood, and the applause thundered as Miles was ushered to the platform to a seat beside Mr. Davis. As he sat down, the great crowd returned to their seats, and the hall became deathly still.

Mr. Davis stood, walked to the lectern, raised his hands and said, "Ladies and gentlemen, we are so pleased to have with us today His Grace, Cardinal Miles Abraham. He prefers to be called Cardinal Miles. He has agreed to help us get through this time of chaos and transition. His wisdom and spiritual leadership is greatly appreciated and needed. Our world has been torn apart by what happened the other day, and for that reason, we are so fortunate to have someone of the Cardinal's status to help us. Ladies and gentlemen, I proudly present to you, Cardinal Miles Abraham." He turned with a gesture to Miles and said, "Your Grace, Cardinal Miles."

Miles stood and walked to the lectern. The throng jumped to its feet and the applause thundered on and on. Miles stood there calmly, with a very stern look on his face. It was the face of a man who knows where he is and where he is going, a look of strength. His eyes looked straight at the crowd; his was the look of a notable orator who commands the attention of a large crowd. He raised his hands, and the large assembly sat down and grew silent, even deathly still. Every ear was attentive and every eye was focused upon Miles. He knew he had their complete attention, and he knew they would hang on every word.

He began in a voice that was loud and clear, and his words were very appealing as he said, "Thank you, Mr. Davis, and my fellow citizens, for this invitation and the opportunity for me to come before this important body. I am honored and shall try to the best of my ability, to serve you in whatever way I can. As I said the other day on TV, none of us can understand what has happened because we the people of earth are simply not far enough advanced. At this juncture, our knowledge is far behind other life forms that we now believe surrounds us. There is no way we can understand that power that reached into our world and took so many of our people away. We can see that we are defenseless against them; with their superior knowledge, we are at their mercy. But one thing is for sure, we must move forward and we must continue to develop ourselves. We have come a long way, and our knowledge has greatly increased in the last one hundred years. I believe we are on the threshold of truly great strides in our quest for knowledge, but this terrible thing has shown us just how far behind we really are. We must unite as never before. Unite . . . as one man, and work together. We have the technology and the brain power to explore new things, but first we must stop the conflict among ourselves within our world. We have the technology to place a mark, the bar code of identification on the person of every citizen. With that I.D. we can assure that everyone, everywhere has plenty, and that everyone, everywhere is in their rightful place. We can eliminate poverty; the haves and the have nots, every citizen can be well cared for with their respective needs, regardless, whether it is medical, housing, clothing or food, all can be assured of plenty."

Miles paused, then continued, "We must learn to communicate with each other; we have the technology to overcome the language barriers through voice unscramblers until we can establish the one universal language. I believe also that the language should be English. If we can bring our world together as one man, who knows what we will learn and develop in time. I wish that today we had the knowledge and the power to go after our departed loved ones and bring them back, but the sad fact is, we do not. That power that took them away can toy with us as it pleases, and who knows what we will face in the future."

Miles paused again and stood looking at his audience, as if to give time for what he was saying to sink in. He was very pleased with himself; he had come to a wonderful time in his life. He continued, "We must have a one-world government with a common monetary system, and we can have that also with the technology that is in existence. We must have a common weapons system, powerful enough to keep the peace. A weapons system such as we saw demonstrated the other day will keep the peace by force here on earth, but it must be controlled by the government of the entire world."

"This, whatever it was, that reached into our world and took so many of our citizens away, must be researched. We must discover the key to life as we know it here on earth, and as whatever that was, has demonstrated. I honestly believe the Star Track transmitter concept is a reality. Now we must discover the power that configures our atoms together, and makes up the things we can see. Our loved ones have been transmitted into another realm. It has been suggested that this great disappearance of our loved ones was the Rapture of God. I do not believe that my God, the God I have served all my life, would do that. This, whatever it was, took all little babies and all small children from their mothers, fathers and their grandparents in a moment. Our own dear Pope was taken out along with millions of others. My God is a God of love and He would not do that. This is the worse blow to mankind here on earth that has ever been. It is so sad. My mail has been jammed, and my phone has been flooded with calls. People are grief stricken in a magnitude that has never been. I say again, my God is a God of love. I cannot believe He would do that to a world He created and loves. This has to be from another source. We are far enough advanced to know that our bodies are made up of atoms, we have come that far, but what is the energy that holds our atoms in the configuration, as we see ourselves today? We must unlock these mysteries; we have been brought to the rude awaking that there are others who have, and they were able to come and take a large number of our people away and there was not a thing we could do about it, but weep and mourn the loss. This is war on a far greater scale than that by Adolph Hitler and the Japanese in World War II. We overcame that, and we learned many things; we will overcome this thing that is so troubling today. I'm convinced we have only touched the hem of the garment in our quest for knowledge."

The huge assembly leaped to its feet and the applause was like thunder. Miles knew he was saying what they wanted to hear, and he knew within himself he was going over big; he was very proud! He let the applause go on and on, finally after about two full minutes he raised his hands and all became silent again, and everyone sat back down.

"I believe something similar to the Constitution of

the United States should be established and be implemented into United Nations. That constitution was designed for a government, of the people, for the people, and by the people, and I believe it should be the foundation upon which we start. That form of government, as far as I am concerned, has proven to be the greatest on the face of the earth. With our modern methods of communicating, we should be able to bring all together as never before, and make things even better. Fellow citizens, today is the day of a new beginning, it is a day of change. What happened the other day has forever changed our world, but it's not the end of our world, we can make it a better world."

Again the great throng leaped to its feet and the applause became a roar. Miles knew he was well on his way and he knew this was his hour to take charge and to do the things he believed should be done. He was saying what they needed to hear; it was something to create a vision of a new and better, safer world. He let the applause go on and on. This time after about one full minute he raised his hands and all became silent again, and everyone sat back down.

Miles continued, "I suggest we adjourn for the rest of this week, each go to his own place, and by prayer, meditation, and good common sense, we put together what we believe in our hearts will work, what we believe will be the best for this body and our world as it is today."

"When we come back together again, we can have input from everyone. May I suggest to you that we establish a governmental structure that will consist of a President, a Vice President, then representative people, one from each of the leading strong nations, to act more or less as the Advisory Board. In addition to those, we can have a House of Representatives that will consist of one person from each of the nations, and one from every religion. That will give us a voice from everyone."

Again the assembly jumped to its feet and applauded. The applause went on and on. Miles stepped back and Mr. Davis took the lectern. After about three minutes he raised his hands and the crowd grew silent and all sat back down.

Mr Davis began, "We have heard these suggestions, do I have a motion that we adjourn?"

There was a very loud voice over the sound system, "Mr Davis, I make a motion we adjourn, but before we do, let's elect his Grace, Cardinal Miles Abraham, to act as our interim President until we get things established." Everyone leaped to their feet again and the applause exploded. Mr. Davis said, "Would you be seated please. You have heard the motion, do we have a second?"

"I second the motion", came a loud voice over the house sound system.

"All in favor stand." Again everyone stood to their feet and the applause went on and on again. Mr Davis motioned to Miles and he stood with Mr. Davis. When Miles raised his hands everyone settled back into their seats again.

Miles began, "Thank you friends, for this vote of confidence. I shall do my best to lead us into the promised land. Thank you so very much. We will come together again next Monday at 9:30 a.m. You are dismissed for now." With that, he turned to Mr. Davis.

The security people moved over to Miles and stood by him as many people rushed on the platform to shake his hand. He made his way down onto the floor and through the crowd, shaking hands, saying, "Thank you, thank you." Finally, several security people completely surrounded him and escorted him to his waiting limousine, and he was taken back to his hotel.

In the hotel, Miles was relieved, he was away from his office and that phone. He had the rest of the week to relax and work on his next move. He could still be reached by phone, but he knew all his calls would be screened. At noon he realized he was hungry, so he called the desk and had a wonderful lunch brought up. He sat alone and ate, he didn't even turn on his TV. After his lunch he took a long nap and was fully relaxed. When he awoke he showered and shaved and spent the rest of the day studying and thinking about the events of the day. He called in his secretary and instructed her on what he wanted his staff to work on. He insisted that he not be disturbed except for a matter of the utmost importance. All incoming calls were to be screened through her.

Miles spent the next two days relaxing; it was wonderful, he had been so pressured over the last few days! He took long naps in the afternoon and when he arose he showered and shaved, and called for food.

On the third day after his lunch he decided to call the Vatican. He realized it was late there, but he was anxious to see how things were going.

He picked up the phone, and a very pleasant female voice answered, "Yes, how may I help you?"

"Please, put me through to the Vatican."

"Thank you sir, one moment please."

He heard the phone switching, then the ring, then, "This is the Vatican operator, how may I help you?"

"Operator, this is Cardinal Miles, please put me through to Cardinal Polenski," Miles answered.

He heard the phone clicking again, then the ring, then the voice answered, "Hello, Cardinal Polenski here."

"Hello Father, this is Father Miles."

"Yes, hello, your Grace. I have been watching the news. I think it's wonderful the way things are shaping up. Congratulations on your new appointment, but Father, have you seen the news from Jerusalem? There are real problems there. According to the report I've received, they estimate there were about a hundred and forty four thousand Jews who claim they saw a vision of the Lord in the air and that He spoke to them, and told them what to do. They are calling us, and all churches, Anti-Christian. They say, according to the teaching of the Bible you are the Antichrist. They are going everywhere waving their Bibles and quoting Scriptures. Also, there are two old men, two old preachers who were on TV, and you would not believe the things one of them said! He said, we are now in a seven-year tribulation period, and that the world will be brought under a one-world system, with the Antichrist at it's head. Also, he says this new system will cause everyone everywhere to receive a mark in their hand or on their forehead before they can buy or sell. He gave the reference in the Book of The Revelation. I looked it up and that's what it says. Father, I sure don't understand all this!"

"He went on to say that God is sending all of us a strong delusion so we will believe a lie and be damned because we have not accepted the Lord Jesus Christ as our personal Saviour. He gave reference from the Bible like the hell fire and brimstone preachers used to do. I'm troubled by all this Father, and frankly I'm worried."

"The news also said that thousands of people are turning and crying to the Lord to save them. It is causing a great stir; I can see enough to know if this continues and grows, our world will really come apart."

Miles was very angry and disgusted, as he said, "Father, I agree this will do harm, but there is just not much we can do about it at this time. I'm going to be tied up here for several days. Issue an official statement from the Vatican and let it read as follows: 'We, of the Catholic Faith, believe in Jesus and the Virgin Mother. Our Church was founded upon the teachings of Jesus by Peter the Apostle. He was our first Pope, and the Lord gave to him the keys to life eternal. The Church has stood the test of time for almost two thousand years. No other church can say that. We shall continue to stand and contend for the truth.' If you will, draft this statement, fax it to me and I'll sign it and send it back. We shall try to mail a copy of it to every living human being on the face of the earth. I believe I have, or can gain access to that mailing list. This will serve as the official stand of the Church. This group of trouble makers will die out in due time. Look at how many have come and gone over the years, but our Church still stands, and is stronger today than ever before."

Miles paused as if he was trying to collect his thoughts, then he said, "In your speaking, Father, warn the people about following those who seek to destroy the unity of the body, rather than trying to build it up. But we must realize there have always been those who would destroy the unity if they could."

"Thank you, Father, I feel so much better after talking to you. You are so wise and so strong."

"Remain steadfast, and continue to carry on, Father, I'll talk to you again tomorrow. Just remember, we have a great cause." with that, Miles hung up.

Miles turned on his TV; there was a news special on. The cameras were focused on the steps of the newly erected Jewish Temple inside the walls of Jerusalem. Miles knew he was watching a tape from an earlier broadcast that had gone out live all over the earth.

Two old men were standing on the steps behind the microphones; one was large, over six feet, very erect.

The other was short, somewhat stooped, a very humble looking person. The camera panned the crowd and thousands could be seen, standing before them listening. As the camera zoomed in on the large one, Miles could see he was probably in his late seventies. He had a very stern look on his somewhat handsome face. His eyes were like steel, and he looked straight into the camera. There was no sign of fear nor confusion in his face. Something about him was almost superhuman and it made Miles want to hear what he had to say.

The large one began in a voice that was very gripping, appealing and almost pleading, "My beloved, I stand here today because . . . I am . . . a Prophet of the Lord. I speak to you the Words of God, and I shall try with everything within me to open your eyes to the truth."

"God said to Israel a long time ago, as He closed out the Old Testament of our Bible. I quote from, Malachi 4:5,-*Behold, I will send you Elijah the Prophet before the coming of the great and dreadful day of the Lord: And he shall turn the hearts of the Fathers to the Children, and the heart of the Children to their Fathers, lest* (before) *I come and smite the earth with a curse.*"

"When Jesus was on earth, some four hundred years later, the ones who were students of the Scriptures, asked Him if He was that Elijah. He answered them as is recorded in Matthew 11:13-15, *All the prophets and the law prophesied until John. And if ye will receive it, this is Elijah, which was to come. He that hath ears to hear, let him hear.* What Jesus said was, The Word of God, the Bible, if you will hear it, that is the Elijah that was to come."

"I'm one of the Prophets. My friend and I are spoken of in the Bible, in The Revelation. We were left the other day after the Rapture, to speak the Words of the Prophets, and of the Law at this time. Our ministry shall only last one thousand two hundred and sixty days, and then you will kill us. Many of you under the sound of my voice this day will believe our words, and accept Jesus Christ as your own personal Saviour. God for Christ sake will forgive your sin, open your eyes, and enable you to see."

"Others of you will reject the Words. I want to say to you . . . this is the last time . . . God's hand of mercy is extended to you. He is not willing that any should perish, but His wrath is going to be poured out without mixture. You . . . will wind up in the Lake of Fire! in everlasting torment, where the worm dieth not, and the fire is never quenched! At this point in time I don't know what that will be, but there is one thing I do know, I certainly do not want to go and spend eternity there."

"For the next seven years there shall be a time of trouble such as never was and shall never be again. The seven year period will be divided into two periods of three and one half years of time. The first is the Tribulation in which there shall be a strong delusion, and seemingly a Utopia. The second will be the Great Tribulation. I feel sorry for those of you who will be alive at that time."

"What happened the other day was that God took the ones who were trusting in Christ, and all little babies and small children under the age of accountability out of this world, and they are now with Jesus in the heavens. It happened as we were told by Jesus that it would happen. Jesus said in, Matthew-24:37-42, and I quote,-*But as the days of Noe were, so shall also the coming of the Son of man be. For as in the days that were before the flood they were eating and drinking, marrying and giving in marriage, until the day that Noe entered into the ark, And knew not until the flood came, and took them all away; so shall also the coming of the Son of man be. Then shall two be in the field; the one shall be taken, and the other left. Two women shall be grinding at the mill; the one shall be taken, and the other left. Watch therefore: for ye know not what hour your Lord doth come.*"

"This is plain, simple, concise language, spoken by Jesus himself. Why there are those of you who are reluctant to believe it, is a mystery to me. How anyone can say, "we don't understand what has happened," *is the mystery of iniquity.*"

"I stand here today and declare unto you that God has done what Jesus said would be done: those who believed in Christ as their Saviour were taken, and those who did not believe, but were trusting in themselves, were left, and you remain here today. Only God knows who you are and where you are, but make no mistake, He knows the heart of every man, woman, boy and girl. He is the eternal, omnipotent God, and He knows everything. He has always been, and He shall always be. Believe . . . on the Lord Jesus Christ, God's son, while there is time!"

"Many are confused about the coming of the Lord, not knowing that His coming was to be in two phases. He has come in the air as a thief in the night and the believers were caught up; that was the first phase."

"After seven years, He will come as the light comes out of the east and shines even unto the west. At that time, every eye shall see Him; that is the second phase."

"Both phases of His coming are referred to and clearly laid out in the twenty-fourth chapter of Matthew, and confirmed in The Revelation."

"The Apostle Paul explained the rapture in detail to the Church, and again I quote, I Thessalonians 4:16-17, *For the Lord himself shall descend from heaven with a shout, with the voice of the archangel, and with the trump of God: and the dead in Christ shall rise first: Then we which are alive and remain shall be caught up together with them in the clouds, to meet the Lord in the air: and so shall we ever be with the Lord.* Again Paul wrote of this event and I quote, 1 Corinthians 15:51-58, *Behold, I shew you a mystery; We shall not all sleep, but we shall all be changed, In a moment, in the twinkling of an eye, at the last trump: for the trumpet shall sound, and the dead shall be raised incorruptible, and we shall be changed. For this corruptible must put on incorruption, and this mortal must put on immortality. So when this corruptible shall have put on incorruption, and this mortal shall have put on immortality, then shall be brought to pass the saying that is written, Death is swallowed up in victory. O death, where is thy sting? O grave, where is thy victory? The sting of death is sin; and the strength of sin is the law. But thanks be to God, which giveth us the victory through our Lord Jesus Christ. Therefore, my beloved brethren, be ye stedfast, unmoveable, always abounding in the work of the Lord, forasmuch as ye know that your labour is not in vain in the Lord.'*

"My beloved, that is exactly what has happened! The phenomenal disappearance was . . . the Rapture . . . Wake up! . . . Wake up! God is not playing games . . . many of you are dangling by a thin thread; dangling by one heart beat over the everlasting Lake of Fire, God's wrath . . . Please, while there is time, wake up!"

"Already there is a false Utopian system being set up. They do not know, nor are the ones left in this world aware of the prophecy of Daniel:-9:26- *'And the people of the prince that shall come shall destroy the city and the sanctuary.'* Titus, the son of the Roman emperor Vespasian, did in fact destroy Jerusalem and the Temple in 70 A.D. Then under Constantine the Great, about 200 A.D, Christianity became the religion of the Roman Empire, and the Catholic church in 1800 years has spread its influence to the four corners of the earth.

This man Miles Abraham is now the head of the hierarchy and he is now the president of the United Nations. He is truly the fulfillment of that prophecy; he is the Prince that was to come, but he is totally blind to the Spiritual things of God. He is as the Scribes and Pharisees were when Christ was on earth; blind to the working of the Spirit of God. Many things about him are prophesied in the Bible For instance the Bible says, and I quote, Daniel 11:36-38, *And the king* (prince) *shall do according to his will; and he shall exalt himself, and magnify himself above every god, and shall speak marvellous things against the God of gods, and shall prosper till the indignation be accomplished: for that that is determined shall be done. Neither shall he regard the God of his fathers,*(the Jews), *nor the desire of women, nor regard any god: for he shall magnify himself above all.* By the teachings of this prophecy the common belief has always been, that this person will be a Jew, and that he will come out of Rome. Beloved this is all a part of the delusion under the Man of Sin, the Prince or King that shall come, the Anti-Christ." The old Prophet paused and looked long and hard at the crowed. Yet there was a tone of compassion in his voice as he continued, "The Apostle Paul said, and again I quote: II Thessalonians 2:3-12, *Let no man deceive you by any means: for that day shall not come, except there come a falling away first, and that man of sin be revealed, the son of perdition; Who opposeth and exalteth himself above all that is called God, or that is worshipped; so that he as God sitteth in the temple of God, showing himself that he is God. Remember ye not, that, when I was yet with you, I told you these things? And now ye know what withholdeth that he might be revealed in his time. For the mystery of iniquity doth already work: only he who now letteth will let, until he be taken out of the way. And THEN shall that Wicked be revealed, whom the Lord shall consume with the spirit of*

his mouth, and shall destroy with the brightness of his com-
ing: Even him, whose coming is after the working of Sa-
tan with all power and signs and lying wonders, And
with all deceivableness of unrighteousness in them that
perish; because they received not the love of the truth, that
they might be saved. And for this cause God shall send
them strong delusion, that they should believe a lie: That
they all might be damned who believed not the truth, that
they might be saved. Beloved, this is the Word of God,
not the foolish imagination of some greedy deceitful
man. God has spoken plainly. Our faith is built upon
the word of God, God has told us what we can look for,
and he has shown the world the fulfillment of His
words. Jesus came into the world according to the
Word of God, He died, was buried and rose again according to what was written before of Him. Now people everywhere have been taken out as was written in
the Word of God and it is beyond my understanding
that a thing of this magnitude can be disregarded and
ascribed to something else. Why not just simply believe
the Word of God and turn to Him?"

Miles jumped up, ran over and turned off the TV. He
was so angry he forgot to use his remote control. How
dare that person stand there at that place so dear to the
heart of so many millions, and speak that way!

Miles knew enough about the Bible to know that
some people can make it say almost anything by taking
a verse here and a verse there. He was outraged! He
would deal with that person and fast. After all, he had
the world's power behind him. All he could see was a
man building a powerful following, one that would
cause trouble and interrupt the unity of his plan. Now
was a time of peace, a time to bring things together.
The last thing the world needed was someone rocking
the boat, stirring up the people. He would have to deal
with him someway.

Miles picked up the phone and again called the Vatican.

"This is the Vatican operator, may I help you?"

"Yes, this is Cardinal Miles in New York, who do we have in the church in Jerusalem?"

"Father, I'll have to check, may I call you back?"

"Yes, please do, I'm in my room, you have my number?"

"Yes, Father, I'll get back to you."

Miles waited, with his mind racing. He thought, those damned Fundamentalists, they have always caused trouble. Down through history, time and again they have had to be dealt with. All they have ever done is divide and cause trouble. Now, here is this guy, trying to divide the world before it even has a chance to get together.

The ringing of the phone interrupted his thoughts, he answered, "Father Miles here."

"Father, this is the Vatican operator, we have Cardinal Spilham in Jerusalem. He has been there for several years. Would you like me to put you through to him?"

"Yes, please do."

Miles heard the phone switching, then the ring. "Hello, this is Cardinal Spilham's residence."

"Yes, may we speak to His Grace please?"

"May I ask who is calling?"

"Yes, Cardinal Miles Abraham from the Vatican."

"Oh yes, one moment please."

Miles heard a long pause, then, "Cardinal Spilham here, how may I help you, your Grace?"

"Father, forgive me for calling at this time, but we have a matter that must be addressed. Did you see and hear that outrageous insult on the steps of the Jewish temple, that's on all the news?"

"Yes, Father, and I'm somewhat disturbed by it."

"Father, contact the officials there, and have him

brought in and questioned. He is really trying to disturb the unity, something we don't need at this time. If you can, try to talk to him yourself, and see if he will be reasonable. Some of the things he's saying are just down right insulting."

"I shall try and do all I can to talk to him, your Grace. I saw you on the news and it's wonderful the way you are bringing things together. Con-gratulations on the appointment. Our world certainly needs someone of your moral stature and wisdom at the helm."

"Thank you, Father, please keep me informed." With that Miles hung up and his mind turned to other pressing things.

He had a copy of the Constitution and the Bill of Rights of the United States brought in. He put his staff in motion to work up something similar to it to serve the new world system. By the time Monday morning came they had drafted documents that Miles felt were well suited to accomplish what he had in mind. He believed he knew what would best serve the people. It was his desire to end strife, war, crime, misery, hunger and the like. He truly believed Utopia could be accomplished.

3

UNITED NATIONS ESTABLISHED

Miles was ushered into the assembly of United Nations at precisely 9:30 Monday morning. As he entered there was a loud voice over the sound system, "The President of United Nations, his Grace, Cardinal Miles Abraham." The people stood and the applause thundered as he was escorted down the main aisle and onto the platform, where he was seated beside Mr. Davis. The applause was still going as he sat down. Mr. Davis stood and raised his hands. It grew quiet and every one was seated.

Mr. Davis began. "My fellow citizens and distinguished guest, I am happy to be back before you this great day. I believe this is a day that will live infinitely. This is a day of a new beginning, a time when our world comes together under a world system that will change forever the way we all live. Here, to lead us through this critical transition, is my very good friend and fellow citizen, the President of United Nations, his Grace, Cardinal Miles." He bowed and made a gesture to Miles. As Miles stood, the assembly stood and again the applause roared like thunder. Miles stood at the lectern, very calm and relaxed. He knew where he was, what he was doing, and what he was going to say. He had prepared with all his ability and intellect for this morning. He knew this morning would either launch his career, or that it would come to an abrupt end if he did not say the right words. The news of the stir in Jerusalem had affected the thinking of a lot of people, and now his credibility was in question by some. Finally, after two full minutes, he raised his hands. The applause stopped and everyone sat back down. There was a deathly calm as he began..."Fellow citizens, Mr. Davis, and distinguished guest, I am happy we have come to this hour in our lives. I believe we are on the fringe of making our world a heaven on earth."

"Over this past week, my staff and I worked day and night to put together suggestions of things we believe will work for this body. This body can be the government of the people, by the people and for the people of the entire world."

"The things I'm going to say are only suggestions, things to be considered, and perhaps acted upon by this body. I would love to see our final design acted upon, first by this body, and then ratified by the entire world, every nation and tongue. I would love to see our world standing, pulling together as one man."

"First, I ask you to hold your applause, please don't interrupt me as I set forth these suggestions. If you will show me this courtesy, it will be greatly appreciated."

"To begin, we believe it is time to have a one-world system of government, with a common monetary system, a common language, a common weapons system and simple laws that will apply to all. The same law for all, regardless of color, race, sex or creed. We can all be citizens of United Nations. Our government can be simple: a President, a Vice President and ten Advisors, one from each of the leading nations at this time. This group will be the Executive Board with veto power and the final vote on any matter. A House of Representatives, consisting of one person from every nation at this time, and one person from every form of Religion, regardless of doctrine, idea or opinion. Each of these key people will have a staff of their choosing to be ratified by the Executive Board."

"We have drafted a modified version of the Constitution and the Bill of Rights of the United States of America, for consideration. It is my desire that we each take these documents and spend time going over them very carefully. Each and everyone should feel free to express their thoughts, and out of this we will come up with the will of this body. I believe we can agree to disagree on things and do what is right for the sake of our world we are shaping. The final documents will not be the will and thinking of one man, but rather the thinking of us all and therefore it will have the support of all.

Allow me to begin with this, with the technology of bar coding, we can have inventory on every citizen. This affords many advantages, I shall list a few: from the day of birth to the day of death, the government will be able to account for each citizen. With a common monetary system, the government will be able to assure food, clothing, housing, medical, and all other needs of every citizen. This will be a simple thing to implement, a simple bar code mark in the palm of the hand or on the forehead if no hand exists. With the satellite links that are set in place at this time, and the world bank, it can be accomplished and on line in a short time, say a little over three years."

"What all this involves is this: we abolish all existing governments, we all become citizens of The United Nations, we will be one, the world over! We put under the control of the United Nations the great weapons system of the United States with it's first-strike capability, and abolish all the rest. Out of all nations, we will form a powerful Army, Navy, Air Force and Marines, and maintain that strong force, as a police force to keep peace if required."

"I suggest we adopt English, as the universal language. It will be tough on some at first, but after a few years it will settle down and become common, as will all the races. Interracial marriage and integration will be encouraged. We will all speak the same words, have the same goals, look the same and act the same, and our world can become a heaven on earth. Financial worries will be gone. A place to live will no longer be a burden. The worry over food and medical attention will no longer be a concern. It can be a world where happiness, contentment and security reigns supreme, a true utopia. The system will not take away the potential of the individual, for instance, if a young person wants to become a doctor, the system will provide the means for him to become the best doctor. If a person wants to study physics, then we will provide the best schools. People of all walks of life will be able to accomplish their desires."

"We have a lot of work ahead of us; there are so many things that remain a mystery. For instance, it is commonly believed the atom is the basic building block of all matter, that all things we see and know are made up of atoms, but what is the power that holds these building blocks together? Some would have us to believe that power is the power of God, but in my way of thinking, I do not believe that is true. For instance, the other day when so many of our citizens were taken, I cannot believe a God of love would do that. Little babies were snatched out of their mothers', fathers' and grandparents' arms. It seems that about all of our young people from fifteen years and under were taken. The God of love, that I know, would not do that. No! a thousands times No! There is another form of life that inhabits space and time and they have unlocked the key to this great mystery of life. We must pursue and find that knowledge. We can; we were able to unlock the atoms and we have learned so much in this field of science! The challenges are great and it will require great minds. We must free those minds, establish the Think Tanks and fund the research programs. The one-world system can do that. With the bar code inventory we can assure an even keel and the fastest possible pace." Miles paused and the assembly jumped to its feet as one man and the applause was spontaneous.

Miles stood there looking down at them, he knew what he had said was right for the time. He felt all warm and excited within himself; he had come to true greatness. Father Kolas would be so proud of him and he was proud of himself: he had done well, from a little rejected boy on the streets of New York, to the President of the entire world. Truly a Prince.

He raised his hands, and all grew calm again. He said, "Fellow citizens, my staff will cause to be passed among you, a copy of what we have suggested."

The stacks of documents were wheeled in, and every available usher went to work placing a copy in each and every hand. Miles stood, he was very calm and quiet, and just watched, taking his time; he was in no hurry.

When the materials were all passed out, even one for himself and one to Mr. Davis, Miles spoke, "I suggest we adjourn, take these documents home, and study them. We can take the rest of this week. Make notes and suggestions, whatever. Let's come together next Monday morning at 9:30 and begin to elect the proper officers and bring our system together."

He turned with a gesture to Mr. Davis who stood and said, "Thank you, Mr. President, do I hear a motion we adjourn?" There was a loud motion and then a second. Mr. Davis said, "All in favor, please stand." They all stood and the exodus began.

Miles was ushered by the security people to his limousine and driven to his hotel. The security people accompanied him to his suite, and two were posted at his door. He realized his private life was a thing of the past but he loved it. He loved the feeling of power, of prestige, pomp and glory.

He called for food; everything his heart could desire was at his beckoning call.

THE DARKNESS

4

Miles was laid back on his bed, propped up on pillows, relaxing, reading a book, when the phone rang. He laid the book down with a sigh and picked up the phone and answered, "Cardinal Miles here."

A very sweet voice answered, "Sir, this is the operator, we have a Cardinal Spilham from Jerusalem on the line, will you accept the call?"

His sigh turned to excitement as he said, "Yes, please put him through."

He listened as the circuits switched and clicked, then a voice said, "Hello, this is Cardinal Spilham, Your Grace. You will not believe what has happened over here."

"Try me, Father, I'm all ears", Miles answered in a joking fashion.

The Cardinal's voice took on a very concerned, serious tone as he said, "Father, I contacted Israel's government and explained to them our concern over this man who calls himself a Prophet. They are also disturbed. They realize you are willing to confirm a cease fire for them; in fact many of them believe you are their long awaited Messiah who will restore the Kingdom to Israel."

"They agreed to call the old prophet in for questioning. It appears that at that juncture a squad of twelve men with a sergeant, were sent to find him and bring him in. They found him . . . the report is, the old man

35

was sitting on the Mount of Olives, and as they approached, they ordered him to come with them."

"Then the strangest thing happened, he looked hard and mean at them and said, If I be the man of God, let fire fall from heaven and consume all but the sergeant."

"According to the report, it was over in a flash, fire fell and vaporized the twelve. The sergeant was blinded, but he made his way back to headquarters. He was so shaken up he could not speak nor write his report far a time. When he was able to speak, the Army sent out two hundred men to investigate, but the guy was gone, and they could see the results of the fire."

"Father, I don't know what to think about this and I'm worried, This city is turned up side down."

"He has something we don't understand, best let him alone, remain steadfast and continue to carry on. We have a great cause, and I guess we can expect some problems, but we will deal with them in due course". Miles said, frustrated. "Thank you, Father, for calling me. We will keep in touch," with that, Miles hung up.

Miles got out of bed and slipped into a nice robe, walked over and turned on his TV. There was a special news bulletin on, and the camera was focused on the Mount of Olives, on the spot where the twelve men had been vaporized. A very worried, confused commentator was speaking. He was so shaken he forgot his behavior as he said, "This is the damnedest thing I've ever seen . . . fire fell here!". The camera zoomed in on him and the spot. It was plain to see the result of the fire. "These guys were vaporized, there is something about that old codger who calls himself a Prophet, something we sure as hell don't understand. I wonder where he came from?"

At that moment, as the cameras panned, the old Prophet appeared; he was very calm and unafraid as he said, "I'm here."

The camera zoomed in on him, and he looked very stern as he said, "This is the sign of Elijah. Read the Word of God and you will see . . . God is stretching out his hand as never before to lost sinners, speaking through signs, wonders and mighty deeds. Not only is prophecy that was spoken almost two thousand years ago, about the whole world being able to look upon this spot simultaneously, and to hear the sound of my voice, being fulfilled before your eyes, you are witnessing the signs of Elijah. Why . . . will you continue in unbelief and rebellion against God? Christ came to save us; believe on Him and be saved before it is everlastingly to late. Behold!—God will give you another sign; let there be darkness over the entire earth for one full twenty-four hour period."

Instantly it went dark, all over the earth and in the sky. There was a total black-out of the sun, moon and stars; very supernatural! It was as if someone threw a switch. All over the world, people were in shock, afraid and confused. Birds and chickens went to roost, and all animals reacted in a confused manner. They all went to their lairs and caves and their hiding places. All lights that were on light sensors came on, but there was a horrifying feeling about it all. Beyond rationalization, no electrical nor phone services were disrupted, all computers and satellites remained the same, but it was black, like nothing that had ever been seen. The ones who were caught out without light groped in the blackness, and many died from fright. There were many crashes of trucks, cars, boats and small aircraft as the unexpected darkness came upon them.

The scene where the old Prophet stood went dark as there were no lights set up for the TV program. Miles turned off his TV and sat in the darkness for a long time. He wondered within himself, What on earth is going on? This is some kind of intervention from outer space. Either the U.F.O. people, or some other form of life; who knows? But someone is playing games with us. Miles really believed that.

Miles thoughts were disrupted by the ring of the phone. He picked it up and said, "Yes?"

The very pleasant female voice said, "Father, this is the hotel switchboard again, I have Mr Doyle Davis on the phone, will you speak to him?"

"Yes, thank you, please put him through."

A trembling, scared voice spoke, "Your Grace, what do you make of all this? We are flooded with calls about this darkness, what do you think, and what can we say?"

"Mr. Davis, the U.F.O. people or whatever, or who-ever, are playing games with us. This makes us realize we must get our research going or else we are in real trouble; I'm convinced! We will address this issue at our next meeting of United Nations on Monday morning. We need time to study the situation. Tell all callers to stay tuned to the TV, and that there will be a press release on this in a short time." Miles was very bold in his answer. There is just no other answer, this old man is from another realm. He was sent to earth for a purpose, what, who knows. Miles believed if he could not lead the world to overcome him and his power, that there was a good chance life as it had been known, would soon cease to exist. He was certainly not going to stop trying to go forward, he had faith in himself and mankind. He hardened his heart against the old Prophet's teaching of the Bible. In fact, to Miles, the translations of the Bible were questionable.

The darkness lasted for one full twenty-four hour day, then the light came back as mysteriously as it left. The world wondered; some believed the Old Prophet was from God, others believed it was an intervention of U.F.O's, and that the old man was from that unknown

world. Confusion and fear reigned everywhere, except
with the believers in Christ; they were at peace knowing
that God was in control.

5

THE U. N. IN ACTION

When Monday morning came, Miles was awakened by the hotel operator at 6:30 on the dot. "Wake up, Mr. President, it's time to rise and shine. What would you like for breakfast?"

"I would like some good hot coffee, sour dough toast with a little butter, 100% spreadable apricot fruit, a hard boiled egg, some good genuine Dutch cheese, with thin sliced ham. Instruct them to leave it on the table, I'll be busy with my morning ritual."

Miles refused to have help with his personal ritual, with one exception: there was an old lady who was assigned to lay out his clothes, and make sure that shoes, socks, shirts, ties and suits were proper for every occasion. He had laid aside his Cardinal's attire this last week, and was now dressed in very expensive hand tailored suits. He always dressed himself, and took his meals in his room. Starting with that meal he would leave his menu on his tray, telling them what he wanted for the next meal. Everything that his heart desired was provided for him by the hotel.

At 8:45 a.m. he was ready to go, sitting with his hands folded on his lap. He was now Mr. President of the United Nations; the most powerful, and most important person on earth.

At exactly 8:55 a.m., there was a knock on his door and one of the security people entered. "It's time, Mr. President."

He was ushered down to his waiting limousine surrounded by security guards. On the drive over to the United Nation's building, which was only twenty minutes away, there was a car with four men in front, and one with four in the rear, two motorcycles, one on each side. His limousine was black, with United Nations and Mr. President flags on the front fenders. He was driven to the side entrance of the building, ushered into the building and up onto the platform at precisely 9:25 a.m.

Mr. Davis was on the platform when Miles arrived. He arose, extended his hand and said, "Good morning, Mr. President, it's good to see you this morning. I hope you were comfortable this last week."

"Thank you, sir, yes, I was very comfortable. It's wonderful to be here."

At precisely 9:30 a.m., Mr. Davis stood behind the lectern and led the delegates in the pledge of allegiance to the flag of the United Nations. There was a prayer by a Catholic Chaplain, and the Representatives were called to order.

Mr. Davis opened by saying, "Ladies and gentlemen, I'm happy to present to you again, our President, Cardinal Miles", he stepped back and yielded the lectern to Miles. Miles stood, and there was a standing ovation, and the applause thundered. He raised his hands and they all took their seats and became very quiet. Miles began, "Thank you very much, Mr. Davis, and my fellow citizens. I'm honored to be a part of this body, and to be here at this historical time. I suggest without further adieu, we proceed to elect ten people, one, from each of the leading nations. Then, that body can elect the representatives from each nation and all religions, as was suggested last Monday. These elections will serve as nominations, until such time as they can be ratified by a general election. Of course, if there is anyone who has a better or different plan, please stand and make your suggestion known." There were none. All remained very still and calm. Miles hesitated for about two minutes and looked out over the great assembly.

He continued, "I would like to start the process by making a motion that we elect Mr. Davis as the Representative from the United States, and also as Speaker of this House."

Over the sound system came a loud voice,"Mr. President, I second the motion."

"All in favor, please stand." The entire body of people leaped to their feet as one man and the applause thundered.

Miles turned to Mr. Davis who had stood, and extended his hand. "God bless you, Mr. Speaker, I now yield the floor to you." With that, Miles sat down.

Mr. Davis was a professional. He took charge, and led in the selection of the other nine representatives. The representatives were: Mr. Davis of the United States, Mrs. Majors of Great Britain, Mr. Filteau of France, Mr. Wilham of Germany, Mr. Musick of Italy, Mr. Ishikawa of Japan, Mr. Hampton of Canada, Mr. Tipliski of Russia, Mr. Chinn of China and Mrs. Rubin of Israel.

After the selection of the ten was over, everything and everyone settled down and the great assembly grew silent.

Mr. Davis spoke, "I feel a pressing need to discuss our concern over the darkness that transpired the other day. That was phenomenal and we really need to consider it, and make an official statement."

"Mr. speaker, I truly believe that old man who calls himself a Prophet, is from another realm." The voice over the sound system was that of Mrs. Rubin, the representative from Israel. She continued, "I hired a private investigation of the Old Prophet on my own. He lives in the Jerusalem hotel and goes by the name of, The Prophet. No one knows where he came from. The report says he and his helper showed up shortly after so many people disappeared. People are afraid of them and none wants to have anything to do with them. Every transaction they make is strictly cash with the American dollar. They go to the Temple every night about sundown, and the old Prophet speaks to the great crowd that gathers to offer the evening oblation, and to hear him. He's a great speaker and quotes many things from the King James version of the Bible. My government has decided to leave him alone. He has some strange power about him and as I have said, most people are afraid of him. I believe the assumption is justified; he was left here after the invasion of our people. Until we can discover the source of this strange power he has, I think he is best left alone."

"I'm certainly persuaded to agree with that decision", Mr. Davis said. "In fact, is there anyone who has more input about him? If so, please let it be known."

Everyone remained silent and it was apparent that nothing was known about the old man.

"It's then the will of this body that we leave him alone? He has already done as much damage to the system as he can. I realize there will come a time when we will have to deal with him, but first, I believe we should pull out all stops and get on with our research. There has to be an answer as to how he caused that darkness. We have seen some amazing things done by the leading magicians of our world. I don't know how, but I truly believe he has some power of deception. Was it dark, or was he playing with our minds? We know somewhere, somehow, there is a power in existence that could cause all little babies, small children and certain adults to disappear. Is it hard to believe that they can also play with our minds? My fellow citizens, we are facing the unknown and it will remain unknown until we find the key to combat it." Mr Davis paused and looked down at the great assembly of people. There was a spirit of questioning that was very apparent.

What really is going on? was running through Miles' mind.

It was decided that a well-worded press statement would be released, tying the darkness into the phenomenal disappearance of so many people and an appeal to everyone to pull together to unlock the mystery that shrouded the world.

The assembly voted that the think tanks and all available brain power would be set in motion to try and come up with some rational answer. The situation was left at that and Mr. Davis moved the organization very smoothly on into other things.

Miles was given an office within the United Nations building. He settled in, and conducted his affairs from there. His office was joined by a door that led into a large conference room, with a very large oval oak table surrounded by twenty chairs. There were two chairs set in behind each of those twenty, making a seating capacity of sixty, with his overstuffed chair at the head. The beauty of it was beyond words, with the color coordination and balance, along with the soft indirect lighting that could be brightened or dimmed. It was an environment with nothing left to be desired. Miles felt like a king.

Out side his office was his private secretary. Her cubicle opened up into a large complex of twenty desks and behind each desk was a secretary. These people had been assigned by Mr. Davis, as staff to the President. They handled all incoming calls, and screened all matters that were directed to the office of the President. Outside that office complex, was a security station, manned with two security people. The station was on duty twenty-four hours a day, seven days per week. Miles was no longer accessible to the public; everyone and everything was screened by his staff before he could be reached. His life was no longer his own; he was caught in the web of bureaucracy, a system of administration, but he loved it.

When 5:00 p.m. came, he would be ushered to his limousine and taken to his hotel with the same escort of cars and motorcycles. That was his daily routine from 9:30 a.m. to 5:00 p.m. five days per week.

After a busy day, when he arrived back at his hotel, he would take a shower, get into a nice robe and settle back to watch the news. He had time, his dinner was served at precisely 6:30 p.m.

One evening Miles turned on the TV to watch the news, there was a news special on. The commentator was covering the events of United Nations, praising the things accomplished. He said, in a voice that was very proud, "Many things have been accomplished in a short time, things that affect the lives of us all. I would like to recap some of the highlights, and I want to thank our wonderful President for his wisdom, and his kindness to all. Folks, I truly believe, for the first time in the history of man, since Adam and Eve were driven from the Garden of Eden, we, of our world, are going to obtain Utopia; it is truly remarkable."

"First, ten people were elected: one from every leading nation, to serve as the Advisory Board with the President. The well-known Mr. Doyle Davis was elected as Representative from the United States and also as Speaker. Secondly from every nation and every major religion, regardless of creed, profession, doctrine, dogma or persuasion, one person will be elected from each, to serve as the House of Representatives. These election all will be interim, until a general election of the people can be held. All existing nations are scheduled to be dissolved as they are today, and will become state/nations to make up United Nations. We will now have one government of the people, for the people and by the people all over the earth. There will be a common monetary system, administered by use of the bar-code, established with an inventory, with an allotment to every citizen. All will have plenty and none will be left out in the cold. With the extending of the hand, all transactions can be finalized in a split second."

"The powerful weapons system of the United States, with it's first-strike capability is being adopted as a peace-keeping force, led by a commander from what is now the United States. As the supreme commander and chief, the President of United Nations will fill that office. All other weapons systems will be dissolved. It is estimated that three years will be needed to inaugurate this system."

"The thing to do now, is that we, the citizens, need to work together to do every thing in our power to bring this about for the good of all mankind."

"The process of setting all this in place, with all the representatives, is slow and very difficult; there have been some disagreements. Egypt does not want Israel to have the land God promised to Abraham. The General Assembly has made every effort to confirm Israel's right to the land, also her right to offer the Evening Oblation in the Temple at Jerusalem."

"There are other factors of differences. Neither France nor China want to surrender their weapons systems, nor their governments to United Nations. There are battles over the monetary system, and the bar-coding."

"There are still other problems, two old men in Jerusalem are kicking up quite a fuss. We will have more on them when we come back after this break."

After the advertising break, the commentator came on again, "Folks, we go now to a tape of events earlier today."

The scene switched to Jerusalem, to the steps of the Temple. Standing on the steps behind microphones, were the two old Prophets. The large one spoke, "Beloved, we have come before you again to speak about matters that are taking place. God has said in II Thessalonians-2:3,-*Let no man deceive you by any means!* My fellow human beings, the whole world is being deceived. God said to Daniel, a long time ago in-Daniel-9:26-27-*'And the people of the PRINCE THAT SHALL COME shall destroy the city and the sanctuary; and the end thereof shall be with a flood, and unto the end of the war desolations are determined. And HE shall confirm the covenant with many for one week: and in the midst of the week he shall cause the sacrifice and the oblation to cease, and for the overspreading of abominations he shall make it desolate, even until the consummation, and that determined shall be poured upon the desolate.'*

"The Romans, did in fact destroy Jerusalem around 70 A.D., which was some 700 + years later. The man that has been elected President of United Nations, is out of what is left of Rome, the Roman Catholic Church, therefore he is That Prince. That is plain to see. God is fulfilling His word before the eyes of the entire world. You will notice also, God said, *He will confirm the covenant with many for one week*. The week is a week of years, seven years. Plainly and simply, this means he is going to say to the Jews, that they have every right to offer the oblation in this Temple as they are doing, and that they have right to the land that God promised to Abraham. But after three and one half years he will break his word, take over this Temple. and set himself up as God."

"My friends, this is not a figment of my imagination, this is what God told Daniel would happen."

"John said in The Revelation, two thousand years ago, and I quote from, The Revelation-13:16-18, *And he causeth all, both small and great, rich and poor, free and bond, to receive a mark in their right hand, or in their foreheads: And that no man might buy or sell, save he that had the mark, or the name of the beast, or the number of his name. Here is wisdom. Let him that hath understanding count the number of the beast: for it is the number of a man; and his number is Six hundred three-score and six.*"

"He (*The Prince*) will cause all men everywhere to receive a mark in their hand or in their forehead before they can buy or sell. That mark is the bar code, that has been proposed."

"John also said,-*Here is wisdom, let him that has understanding count the number of the beast: for it is the number of a man: and his number is 6,6,6.*"

"We know that what God calls Beasts are spiritual systems of men. We are told this plainly by the angel in Daniel, and I quote from Daniel-7:15-17, *I Daniel was grieved in my spirit in the midst of my body, and the visions of my head troubled me. I came near unto one of them that stood by, and asked him the truth of all this. So he told me, and made me know the interpretation of the things. These great beasts, which are four, are four kings, which shall arise out of the earth.*"

"Also the beast sometime is spoken of as a man. When we consider this, we know we cannot have a system of government without a man, and a man who is recognizable is a man of a system, so therefore spiritually speaking the two are one and the same."

"In God's spiritual numbering system, "7", is the number of God, "6", is the number of man, the 6, 6, 6, means the system will be a government of man (6), by man (6) and for man (6). Oh! . . . beloved mankind, God is showing us these things, confirming the Prophecy of His Word. These are things we see and should be able to understand. There has been so much written about 6, 6, 6, being the mark of the beast. 6, is not a mark, it is a number, I will repeat 6, 6, 6, is the number of the Antichrist system of Government. His mark will be the bar-code and he will cause all who refuse it to be put to death"

There was a knock on the door; it interrupted the program, so Miles turned off the TV and answered the door.

"Your dinner, sir", and the cart of food was wheeled into his room. Oh, well, it didn't matter, he had heard all of that old man he wanted for one day.

After dinner he lay back and took a long nap in an easy chair. It was a habit he had adopted from Father Kolas so long ago. He smiled to himself as he thought of the old Father, the way he would lay back and snore after his evening meal.

Miles lay there a short time, but his thoughts troubled him. He had to do something to shut that old man up, or at least discredit him. He was, "digging under his wall", and really getting under his skin. Miles almost had the power of the entire world behind him, there had to be some way to make the old man understand how wrong it was to divide the body, and disturb the unity. Someone has to be in charge, and it so happens, I am the man in charge. Oh well, I will do what has to be done tomorrow, he thought. Miles had learned to take things one day at a time.

He went to his beautiful bed and drifted into a deep sleep, and as he slept, he dreamed of an extraordinary world government, where all the citizens were cared for, a world government with electronic money, so that, if more money was needed, it could be appropriated. No longer would there be the poor and needy, or the homeless; it would be Utopia.

He awoke and lay for a long time planning and thinking of ways to make this dream come true. It was the desire of his heart that all should have plenty and that there should be peace among men.

He couldn't go back to sleep, so he decided to turn the TV on. He hit the remote and the TV. slowly lit up and the picture came into focus. The program was coming from the steps of the Temple in Jerusalem and Miles was surprised the smaller of the two Prophets was speaking. His voice was soft and he presented himself as being a very intelligent person. Something about him caused Miles to want to hear what he had to say. This was the first time Miles had heard him speak; he was usually standing very quietly in the background. He was speaking in a very pleasing fashion, very slowly, and his words were very clear.

"My friends, this evening I'm trying to show you what has happened in the history of the Church. Maybe this message will shed some light, and some of you will be convinced that we two prophets are speaking the truth. When Jesus died on the cross somewhere around 33 AD, his eleven remaining disciples were very distressed. They did not know what to think. They had believed He was the long awaited Messiah, and had come into the world to establish the long overdue Kingdom to Israel. When He was crucified that really threw them; they just simply did not know what to think. After the death of Jesus, they still assembled together, and the resurrected Jesus started appearing to them. They realized He had in fact risen from the dead. He showed himself alive for some forty days, then one day, as they were all together, they asked him, Will you restore again the kingdom to Israel?"

Jesus answered, "It is not for you to know the times or the seasons which the Father has put in his own power. But you shall receive power, after that the Holy Ghost is come upon you; and you shall be witnesses unto me both in Jerusalem, and in all Judea, and in Samaria, and unto the uttermost part of the earth."

After He had spoken these words, they all walked together out to the Mount of Olives. He said to them, "All power is given unto me both in heaven and in earth. Go ye therefore, and teach all nations, baptizing them in the name of the Father, and of the Son, and of the Holy Ghost. Teaching them to observe all things whatsoever I have commanded you: and, lo, I am with you always, even unto the end of the world. Amen." While they looked at Him, suddenly he began to rise, and a cloud received Him out of their sight. They stood dumbfounded, looking up into heaven. Seemingly out of no where, standing with them were two men dressed in shinning white garments, and one of them said, "You men of Galilee, why do you stand looking up into heaven? This same Jesus, which is taken up from you into Heaven, shall so come in like manner as you have seen him go into heaven", and then they were gone.

The disciples returned to Jerusalem as Jesus had told them to do, and waited until the Holy Spirit was sent to help them. Through and under the direction of the Holy Spirit, the Church was established: and church history is a matter of record unto this day."

"Tonight, I want to look at the history of the Church in the light of what was prophesied in The Revelation almost two thousand years ago. The Revelation opens with this, *'The Revelation of Jesus Christ which God gave to him, to show to His servants things that must shortly come to pass; and He sent and signified it by his angel unto His servant John.'* That verse my beloved, is the key to the book of The Revelation. God has shown his servants things that we can see, things that we can know, and if there was nothing else, that fact alone makes us know the God of our Bible lives. We find in the first three chapters the message is directed to the Church. That's the Church over-all, the Church reflection in the world, what man can see. This message to the church is broken down into seven periods of time, or seven different stages in the history of the Church. It is symbolically given by using seven local churches that were in Asia Minor at that time. It is believed the book of The Revelation was written by John the Apostle around 96 AD. The seven churches were: Ephesus, Smyrna, Pergamos Thyatira, Sardis, Philadelphia and Laodicea. The first of these was Ephesus, and it signified the desirable time and covered a place in history from AD 33 to around 100-AD. The second was Smyrna which means, Myrrh, which was associated with death. That covered a time in history from 100 to around 312 AD. The time of the great percussion by six bloody rulers of Rome. The third was Pergamos which means marriage. That covered the time of the Church from around 313 to 606 AD. The time when the marriage was formed between the Church and the Roman Empire. The forth was Thyatira which means continual sacrifice. That was the overall reflection of the Church during that time from 606 to 1520 AD. When I consider that time I'm always reminded of what Paul said in the book of Hebrews 10:11, *And every priest standeth daily ministering and offering oftentimes the same sacrifices, which can never take away sins.* The fifth Church period was Sardis which means dead. That is the true reflection of the Church's outstanding image from 1520 to 1750 AD. The sixth was Philadelphia which means brotherly love. During that time there was a revival starting with the Reformation and reflects the time from 1750 to a little beyond 1900 AD. The seventh which number stands for God's divine completeness was called Laodicea, which means lukewarmness, nether cold nor hot. Christ's last message to the church age is recorded in The Revelation, 3:15-22, and I quote, *I know thy works, that thou art neither cold nor hot: I would thou wert cold or hot. So then because thou art lukewarm, and neither cold nor hot, I will spue thee out of my mouth. Because thou sayest, I am rich, and increased with goods, and have need of nothing; and knowest not that thou art wretched, and miserable, and poor, and blind, and naked: I counsel thee to buy of me gold tried in the fire, that thou mayest be rich; and white raiment, that thou mayest be clothed, and that the shame of thy nakedness do not appear; and anoint thine eyes with eyesalve, that thou mayest see. As many as I love, I rebuke and chasten: be zealous therefore, and repent. Behold, I stand at the door, and knock: if any man hear my voice, and open the door, I will come in to him, and will sup with him, and he with me. To him that overcometh will I grant to sit with me in my throne, even as I also overcame, and am set down with my Father in his throne. He that hath an ear, let him hear what the Spirit saith unto the churches.*"

"It's a sad state, as we look at the latter days of the Church. At the beginning, Christ Jesus was standing in the their midst, symbolized by the Golden candlesticks; at the end He was standing on the outside at the door knocking, wanting to come in."

"The third chapter closes the time of the church, and chapter four opens with this, *After this I looked, and, behold, a door was opened in heaven: and the first voice which I heard was as it were of a trumpet talking with me; which said, Come up hither, and I will shew thee things which must be hereafter.* Beloved, that teaches us after the Church had run it's course, the true Church, the believers, were taken out and carried into heaven. That's what happened at the Rapture. These are things that we can see, God told us they would come to pass, and we can see where they have. I'll confess to you I cannot understand unbelief. Let me say again, God has shown us these things and there are many, many things recorded here. At the time they were written they seemed incredible, but today we can see them plainly.'

Miles abruptly turned off his TV, what the man said didn't make sense to him. He believed a person could take these signs and symbols and make almost any thing out of them. But there was one thing for sure he was going to have to deal with those two old trouble makers, he thought.

CARDINAL SPILMAN

6

Miles was in his office at 9:30 a.m. sharp the next morning. He made a decision about the trouble being created in Jerusalem. Something had to be done. He decided the best thing would be to contact Cardinal Spilham in the Jerusalem church, and ask him to handle the situation. He would free his hands and give him the authority to do what had to be done. That old guy who called himself a Prophet was simply going too far.

He picked up the phone, his secretary answered, "Yes, Mr. President, how can I help you?"

"Would you put me through to Cardinal Spilham at the Church in Jerusalem."

He sat and waited as she made the call. She was such a nice person, so beautiful and refined. For a moment he thought how wonderful it would be to have someone like her to share his lonely bed at night. But he killed the thought; he could not regard the desire for women. His life was involved with other things and always had been. From the time he was a little boy until now, he had this burning desire to be where he was, and now he thought, just look where I am! His thoughts were interrupted by the voice, "Go ahead, Mr. President."

"Hello, Cardinal Spilham."

"Hello, Mr. President, how can I be of service to you?"

"Cardinal, I was watching tapes last evening of the

two old men who calls themselves Prophets. I'm concerned over the way they are disturbing and hindering the cause. I was wondering, do you think it would do any good if you had a talk with them?"

"I don't know sir, but we never know until we try. I'll get in touch with them and have a talk."

"Thank you, Cardinal, and let's keep in touch."

Cardinal Spilham went to the Jerusalem Hotel. The folks that ran the hotel had come to Jerusalem from the United States in the late 1800 hundreds. Most of them were taken out by the Rapture, but there were still enough left to staff the old hotel.

Father Spilham had learned that the two old prophets were staying there. As he approached the desk, a very pleasant lady said, "Yes, how can I help you, Father?" He had known these folks a long time.

"Are the two old Prophets staying here, Mrs. Vester?"

"Yes sir, they are, the large one is in room 205, just up the stairs and down the hall on your left, the other one is across the hall in 206."

"Thank you very much," and he turned to the stairs. As he approached the door he had no idea whatsoever what he was going to say, but the President wanted him to talk to this man, so talk he would. He knocked on the door and the old man opened the door.

"Hello, Cardinal, please come in, I've been expecting you."

Cardinal Spilham was shocked as he said, "You have?"

It was as if the old man was looking into the depth of Cardinal Spilham's soul as he said, "Yes, in a dream last night, the Holy Spirit of God revealed to me that you are a chosen vessel, one who will be used of God in a mighty way."

He completely threw Cardinal Spilham off-track. He had not expected something like this.

The old Prophet said, "Come on in, Father, please sit down, the Lord wants me to talk to you."

He began in a voice that was very soft, full of love and compassion as he said, "Cardinal Spilham, Christ died for our sins, you know that, but you have never taken Him as your own personal Saviour, if you had, you would have gone out in the Rapture the other day. Your eyes are closed to Spiritual things. Sir, you need to be born again, God said many years ago, by the Apostle Paul in the book of I Corinthians-2:14, *The natural man receiveth not the things of the Spirit of God: for they are foolishness unto him: neither can he know them, because they are spiritually discerned.* That simply means, unless the Lord gives you a heart to perceive, eyes to see and ears to hear you cannot know God in an intimate way. You must realize, my friend, God wants to live within us and be the most important part of our lives. Man was made for God, and God will dwell within us by His Spirit if we will only open the door."

Cardinal Spilham looked at him and wondered as he said, "You know, I am a Cardinal in the Catholic Church. I've been here for twenty years, standing faithfully for the Church. We believe in Jesus and the Virgin Mary."

"I know that, sir, it is one thing to believe He is in your mind, yet quite another to accept Him in your heart as your own personal Saviour. You are trusting in yourself; what you do, and what you have done, all that is filthy rags in God's sight. We've all sinned and do come short of the glory of God. We must be born again. You are standing before me, as Nicodemus stood before Jesus in the third chapter of John. Just as Jesus said to him, *you must be born again*, even so, I say to you, you must be born again. Once you accept Christ, God for His sake will send the Holy Spirit into your heart. Then and not until then can you know the things of God. Look here in my Bible what God has said, and the old Prophet picked up his Bible from the night-stand beside his bed and turned to Romans, 8:5-17, and read out loud to Cardinal Spilham, *For they that are after the flesh do mind the things of the flesh; but they that are after the Spirit the things of the Spirit. For to be carnally minded is death; but to be spiritually minded is life and peace. Because the carnal mind is enmity against God: for it is not subject to the law of God, neither indeed can be. So then they that are in the flesh cannot please God. But ye are not in the flesh, but in the Spirit, if so be that the Spirit of God dwell in you. Now if any man have not the Spirit of Christ, he is none of his. And if Christ be in you, the body is dead because of sin; but the Spirit is life because of righteousness. But if the Spirit of him that raised up Jesus from the dead dwell in you, he that raised up Christ from the dead shall also quicken your mortal bodies by his Spirit that dwelleth in you. Therefore, brethren, we are debtors, not to the flesh, to live after the flesh. For if ye live after the flesh, ye shall die: but if ye through the Spirit do mortify the deeds of the body, ye shall live. For as many as are led by the Spirit of God, they are the sons of God. For ye have not received the spirit of bondage again to fear; but ye have received the Spirit of adoption, whereby we cry, Abba, Father. The Spirit itself beareth witness with our spirit, that we are the children of God: And if children, then heirs; heirs of God, and joint-heirs with Christ; if so be that we suffer with him, that we may be also glorified together."*

The old Prophet laid his Bible back on the nightstand and said, "You can see by this, Cardinal Spilham, no man can know the things of God, but by the Spirit of God. Friend, you need to call out to Christ to save your soul, open your eyes and come alive within your heart.

Cardinal Spilham realized what he said was true. He knew about God, but in no way did God live within him. He was a man that had always done what the Church told him to do.

He looked at the old Prophet, he knew there was something different about him; he had something he himself, did not have. He said very humbly, almost pleading, "Sir, would you pray for me?"

"Yes, let's kneel here before God, and call upon Him and ask Him to save you."

They knelt beside the old bed, the old Prophet put his arm around Cardinal Spilham's shoulder and prayed, "Lord, you know the heart of every man, you know the heart of this man, this day. Lord, help him to trust you for the salvation of his soul. Help him to understand you died for him. Now Cardinal, will you pray and pour out your heart to the Lord? Ask Him to save you."

Cardinal Spilham began, very sincerely, "Lord, you know me, I know about you, but Lord I've never asked you to save me. Lord save me now, let your blood wash away my sin." Suddenly he began to weep and strangely enough, in his mind, he saw Christ dying on the cross just for him. At that moment he knew God had saved him. All things became new, he did not know how, but he knew what it was to be born again.

They stood together, and he put his arms around this dear old man. His spiritual eyes were open, and he could see things clearly.

The old Prophet spoke, "My brother, you are going to draw a lot of fire from the Church, and from your superiors. You need to spend a lot of time in Bible study. I'll help you all I can. God will enable you to see and understand. I suggest you sit down and read the book of The Revelation. God will reveal many things to you; it is a book given to show God's servants things that must shortly come to pass, but bear in mind, it is given in the spiritual symbolic language of the Bible. If you remember when Jesus was here, He said, in John-5:39,-*Search the scriptures, for in them you think you have eternal life, and they are they that testify of me.*

"Jesus was testified of in the old Testament in symbolic, spiritual language. Read also the book of Daniel; it will shed a lot of light on the things that are happening, and you will see a lot of the symbolic language of the Revelation explained there. God bless you my Brother and if you have questions feel free to ask."

Cardinal Spilham knew he had to go back to the Church and report to President Miles. His whole sequence of thinking had changed. He was a new man, old things had passed away, and all things were new. This was a new beginning for him. He wanted to tell the whole world that Christ had died for him.

He returned to the Church, to his quarters where he had spent the last twenty years. But they were different to him. He realized these things were only temporal. Soon all this would be gone; it had no lasting foundation and it was not eternal. He had put his eyes on things above, and from this day he would live, not for himself, but for the Lord.

He picked up his phone, the operator said, "Yes, Father, how can I help you?"

"Please put me through to President Miles in New York."

"Just a minute, please."

He sat there listening to the phone switch, then the rings. "Hello, this is United Nations."

"Please put me through to President Miles."

"Who is this calling, please?"

"Cardinal Spilham, of the Church in Jerusalem."

"Thank you, one moment please."

"Hello, Cardinal Spilham, did you contact the old Prophet?"

"Yes sir, I did."

"How did it go, will he be reasonable?"

"Mr. President . . . he showed me where we are

wrong. What we are trying to accomplish is not the will of God. It is inspired by Satan, the god of this world, and it is a literal fulfillment of the Word of God."

There was silence . . . Cardinal Spilham knew he had drawn fire. He would be lucky . . . if he only sent him to lower Siberia.

Miles voice was very harsh as he said, "Spilham, what are you saying? This is the worse time possible for you to turn and join that crowd. Think man . . . you are a man of great influence. You will do so much damage to the World System we are trying to establish. Are you sure this is what you want?"

"Yes, Mr. President, I'm sure. I accepted the Lord Jesus as my Saviour and He opened my eyes. I can understand what is happening. You could also, if you would get your heart right with God . . . stop trusting in yourself and going after the things of the flesh."

Now Miles was really angry as he said, "Spilham, that is the most asinine thing I've heard in all my life, Man, you have lost it. You best pack your things, and return to the Vatican."

Cardinal Spilham was so sad, he was almost in tears as he said, "No sir, I will not return to the Vatican. I will vacate these quarters and my position, but I shall remain here. My work is here in Jerusalem, and I'll remain here until I die."

There was click and he knew President Miles had hung up the phone.

Cardinal Spilham left his personal things in his quarters. He called a cab and went back to the Jerusalem Hotel. As he entered, Mr. Vester was at the desk, "Yes, Cardinal, how can I be of service to you."

"I need a room sir, the Vatican has recalled me, I'm no longer Pastor of the Church here."

"What on earth happened?"

"I've accepted Christ as my Saviour. I'll be working for His cause the rest of my life."

Mr. Vester looked at him with a question in his eyes as he said,"Well, I thought you were doing that, and had been for the past twenty years."

"Mr. Vester, if our lives were what they should have been, we would have been taken up in the Rapture. The very fact that we were left makes me know we were trusting in ourselves, and not in the Lord. God knows all hearts, and He has separated the wheat from the chaff. The old Prophet helped me to see that, and I fell on my face before the Lord and asked him to save me."

"Your Grace, I don't want to become entangled in your personal life; we are certainly happy to have you come live here. In fact, the two old Prophets live here, I'll give you a room next to them."

"Thank you, Mr. Vester. Do you have a little truck of some kind, that I can use to get my things out of the quarters at the Church?"

"Yes, and we have a man who will help you. Also, we have a storage space for you if you need it. Would you like to go right away?"

"Yes, I might as well get it over with."

When Cardinal Spilham arrived at the church; where he had served for more than twenty years, he found a divided staff. Miles had called the church and given them his version about what had happened. Father Frank Reevas, who was the 2nd Pastor had already taken charge and informed the staff of Cardinal Spilham's offense.

Cardinal Spillham entered his quarters; there were boxes all over the place and his personal things were being packed.

"So you decided to join the Old Prophet", Father Reevas said in a very belligerent tone.

Cardinal Spilham could see some of the members of

his staff were very troubled and they were weeping, others seemed happy to see him go.

He joined in with the packing and did not answer Father Reevas, in fact he had found him very hard to love at times as he was very worldly for a Priest.

One old lady, Sister Mary, who had served as his house keeper asked, "Father, what is this all about. We have worked together for more than twenty years?"

"Yes Sister, I know, but my views have changed and I was recalled by Cardinal Miles?"

"Why, Father?"

"Sister, I know this is going to shock you, but we've all been doing things through the energy of the flesh. Our hearts were not right with the Lord, had they been; we would have been taken out at the Rapture. Today I realized that, and I've put my faith and trust in Christ and asked Him to save me. When I told Cardinal Miles, he said I was out of my mind, and ordered me to leave here and return to the Vatican. I refused to return to the Vatican; I'm going to spend the rest of my life working with the Christians and the Jews."

"Father I don't understand, you're a good man and you've always served the church with all your heart."

"That's the trouble Sister, I was serving the church and not the Lord."

"I don't understand, Father, I've always thought they were one and the same."

"Sister, if our hearts were right with the Lord, we would no longer be here, but we were left when Jesus called His own unto Himself. But my dear, it is not to late to turn to the Lord with all your heart and ask Him to save you, that's what I did and he opened my blinded eyes. You remember in the Bible Jesus said, in Matthew-7:22-23, *Many will say to me in that day, Lord, Lord, have we not prophesied in thy name? and in thy name have cast out devils? and in thy name done many wonderful works? And then will I profess unto them, I never knew you: depart from me, ye that work iniquity."*

"Those were good people Jesus was talking to, but they were trusting in themselves and their good works. Even so it was when the Rapture came, Jesus separated the saved from the unsaved. I realized today although I had pastored this church for better than 20 years, that did not save me. Sister, I knelt on my knees and asked Jesus to save me and I know he has.

Father Reevas was standing listening; he looked very disgusted as he said, "That's all a lot of nonsense, Father. The quicker we can get you out of here the better. I've never heard such foolishness. Father Miles was right, fellow, you've lost it. Let's get all your stuff together and get you out of here, I don't want you poisoning the minds of these folks, we still have a church to maintain here."

"I'm sorry for all of you Father Reevas, I shall pray for all of you that the Lord will open your eyes. I realize Cardinal Miles wants someone here who will follow him, and I can no longer do that."

Cardinal Spilham could see they did not understand and there was much confusion among them. He realized he no longer belonged there.

As quickly as possible his stuff was loaded onto the little truck and he was driven by the man, back to the hotel. The driver did not say a word; he was not paid to think, he was paid to drive.

Cardinal Spilham moved into the hotel. His room was small but clean. It had everything he would need to make his life comfortable. None of the fancy frills he was used to, but it was adequate. He lay back on his bed, and prayed; it was a trying time, and he had a feeling it was going to get worse.

As he lay staring at the ceiling, he wept. On the one hand he was overjoyed over Christ saving him, but on the other, he had paid a great price. He loved the Church and the people that he worked with and ministered to. Somehow, he realized he would have to pay eventually with his life. As he prayed, there was a peace that passed over him. He realized the Lord was in control, His grace was sufficient and he must learn to trust and lean upon Him. He drifted into a peaceful sleep. As he slept, he dreamed he could see thousands coming to Christ as he had done.

When he awoke, he dressed in a plain suit and stepped out of his room. Just as he did, the old Prophet came out of his room and they met in the hall.

The old Prophet looked surprised as he said, "Hello, Father Spilham, what are you doing here?"

"I just moved in. When I called President Miles and told him about accepting the Lord, he recalled me. I refused to go back to Rome; I'll stay here until the end."

"I knew that would happen. Jesus said, in John-15: 19-24, and I quote, *If the world hate you, ye know that it hated me before it hated you. If ye were of the world, the world would love his own: but because ye are not of the world, but I have chosen you out of the world, therefore the world hateth you. Remember the word that I said unto you, The servant is not greater than his lord. If they have persecuted me, they will also persecute you; if they have kept my saying, they will keep yours also. But all these things will they do unto you for my name's sake, because they know not him that sent me. If I had not come and spoken unto them, they had not had sin: but now they have no cloke for their sin. He that hateth me hateth my Father also. If I had not done among them the works which none other man did, they had not had sin: but now have they both seen and hated both me and my Father.*"

"My Brother, commit these words to memory, you will need to draw strength from them in time to come.

But be of good cheer, greater is He that is in us, than he that is in the world." The old man smiled, and he looked straight and lovingly into Father Spilham's eyes

"I know that, and I'm ready to go all the way for the Lord." Father Spilham answered without hesitation.

"We are having a rally on the steps of the Temple tonight, after the Evening Oblation. Why don't you come and give your testimony?"

"I would love to. What time?"

"The service will start at 8:30 p.m. The Jews offer the Evening Oblation at sundown; after that, I'm going to bring a message. You'll be a great testimony."

At 8:25 p.m. Father Spilham made his way through the great crowd and up to the steps of the Temple. The microphones, cameras and lights were all set in place. He could see it was going to be a televised rally, and he knew it would go out live all over the earth. Many thousands had gathered to hear the old Prophet.

When the Jews finished offering their Oblation, the old Prophet walked up behind the microphones. The lights and cameras were focused upon him. He stood looking into the camera, it was the look of a man who was perfectly at ease and knows exactly what he is doing. There was a calmness and a boldness about him. A hush moved over the great crowd; all were quiet, as he began. "My friends, and fellow citizens, I come before you again tonight, to declare unto you the truth from God. In a few days you are going to be asked to register so you can be bar-coded. *Do not take that mark!* . . . God said in The Revelation, 14: 9-12, *If any man worship the beast* (system) *and his image, and receive his mark in his forehead, or in his hand, The same shall drink of the wine of the wrath of God, which is poured out without mixture into the cup of his indignation; and he shall be tormented with fire and brimstone in the presence of the holy angels, and in the presence of the Lamb: And the smoke of their torment ascendeth up for ever and ever: and they have no rest day nor night, who worship the beast and his image, and whosoever receiveth the mark of his name. Here is the patience of the saints.'*

"*Do not! . . . Do not take that mark!* The day will come when we will have to die for refusing, but beloved of God, that is the price we must be willing to pay. This is a great trial of our faith. Jesus also said, in Matthew-24:13, *He that shall endure unto the end shall be saved.*"

"He is not saved because he endured, rather he endures because he is saved. I ask you tonight, are you saved, are you trusting in the Lord Jesus as your Saviour? If not let me plead with you to accept Him before it is everlastingly to late."

"Beloved, the day is far spent, Christ died on a cross for our sins just outside this city, two thousand years ago. He said, in John-3:18-19,-*He that believeth on Him is not condemned: but he that believeth not is condemned already, because he hath not believed in the name of the only begotten Son of God. And this is the condemnation, that light is come into the world, and men loved darkness rather than light, because their deeds were evil.*"

"Beloved of God, these are not my words, but the words of Jesus, and they came from the very Throne of Heaven."

"You Jews who are offering the Oblation, I realize your eyes are darkened, and you do not see as yet what you are doing. Under the Law, you were to offer sacrifices, but the offering was looking forward to the time when the Lamb of God would be offered. In offerings you were rolling your sin forward, year after year. But when Christ came, He offered Himself, once and for all. His offering of His Blood takes away our sins. God, for His sake, will forgive sin. We Christians sing, 'Jesus

paid it all, all to Him I owe.' Oh . . . beloved mankind",
and tears came streaming down the old Prophets face,
"Why will you not believe God?"

"At the Rapture the other day, God separated the believers from the unbelievers. But you do not have to remain in unbelief; you can turn here tonight and take
him into your heart."

"We have with us tonight a man that many of you
know. He has been pastor of one of the churches here
in this city for twenty years. But being a pastor did not
save him. When the Rapture came he was left, but today, on his knees he asked the Lord to save him. God
heard his prayer, and he is here tonight to tell us about
it. Cardinal Spilham from the Catholic church here in
Jerusalem", and the old Prophet stepped back.

Cardinal Spilham moved to the microphones. He felt
a power and presence that he had never known before,
as he began to speak. He knew within himself the Lord
was speaking through him. He began, "Friends, and all
who are watching, as I stand here tonight, I'm not
alone. Christ through the Holy Spirit, lives within my
heart. He came into my heart and life today. For many
years I've been trusting in myself. I was a Pastor of one
of the greatest churches on earth. I have ministered
about God to thousands, but it was all in the flesh, the
works of the flesh. When the Rapture came the other
day, I knew in my heart something was not right within
me, but God knew my heart. Today, this dear old
brother led me to accept Christ as my Saviour, and to
stop trusting in myself. God, for Christ's sake forgave
my sin, and sent the Holy Spirit into my heart crying,
Aba Father. Tonight I am saved; His Spirit bears witness with my spirit that I am a child of God. Oh! glory
to God, Christ lives within me. I now want to live for
Him. I plead with you here, and under the sound of my
voice, turn to Him before it is too late. God is not will-

ing that any should perish, but that all should come to repentance."

There was a loud shout from the front of the crowd. A man in his early thirties came running up, knocking people out of his way and yelling at the top of his voice, "You bunch of crazy people, our President is trying to pull our world together, and you are tearing it apart with all this dumb preaching." He made a lunge at Cardinal Spilham.

It looked as if the old Prophet spit fire at him. Fire came out of the old Prophet's mouth, and the guy was engulfed in flames. He screamed, ran in circles and fell dead. There was a gasp of horror that moved over the entire watching world.

MR. MIRANDOLA

7

Miles was watching and listening to the entire thing. When the guy fell dead, he jumped up and turned off the TV. That was phenomenal, that old man had something, and Miles was convinced he was influenced from outer space.

He was confused and angry as he picked up his phone.

The very sweet voice of his secretary answered, "Yes, Mr. President?"

In a very stern and enraged tone he said, "Call a meeting of the staff, and the Representatives from the Ten Nations in the conference room at 2.00 p.m.. today."

Miles was so mad he could not eat his lunch. Something had to be done about that guy. Never in all his life had he been so upset. This guy had some kind of secret weapon, and they would have to fight this fire some way.

At 2:00 p.m. everyone was settled in their place in the conference room. Miles took his seat at the head of the table and in a very disgusted fashion asked, "How many of you saw that spectacle from Jerusalem on TV, around noon today?" They all raised their hands; Miles knew they had been watching. It was broadcast as a News Special all over the world.

"People, that scene went out all over the earth, and it is very damaging. We can't afford to sit on this; something has to be done. I have called you together so we can consider this and come to some conclusion on what course of action to take. Any suggestions?"

Ms. Carol Lumbro, one of the secretaries raised her hand, "Mr. President."

"Yes, Carol."

"I know a man; he's a great sorcerer, his name is Mirandola. He took his name from someone out of the distance past and he's considered to be the greatest magician on earth, and he is performing at night, here in New York. I'll contact him, and see if he will help us. If we also can show some phenomenal things; things that people cannot understand. Then with well prepared speeches, maybe we can offset the teachings of these old men."

"Thank you, Carol, that's a good idea. Anyone else have any suggestions?"

"Yes, Mr. President." Doyle Davis spoke up. "Lets speed up the registration and bar-coding. Start in Jerusalem, that way if these old men refuses to register, we can put them in prison and that will eliminate them."

"That's a very good suggestion, Mr. Davis. I believe we have the power to pass a law and make registration mandatory. I don't know about the bar-coding as yet, but we can certainly give it a try. In the meantime we can use Mr. Mirandola to offset some of the things being said. I would love to see his act."

Carol spoke out, "I'll get tickets and make reservations, and maybe we can catch his act tonight, if you like?"

"Thank you, Carol. Why don't we do that, and then we can meet here tonight after the show and discuss this situation further. That's all I have for now. Keep your thinking caps on, thank you, you are dismissed."

They all stood, and one at a time said, "Thank you, Mr. President", and they all left.

Miles sat there a long time and wondered. Down deep inside, he was troubled, confused and uncertain. Yet, it seemed that some force from within was driving him on. He had to bring all this under control, regardless of what it took. His thoughts were interrupted by the phone. He picked it up,"Yes."

"Mr. President, I have Ms. Lumbro on the line."

"Thank you, I'll take it."

"Hello, Carol."

"Hello, Mr. President. I spoke to Mr. Mirandola, and made all the arrangements for us to have a front row seat at his performance tonight. Moreover, he will be glad to return with us after the entertainment, and talk about how he can be helpful to us at this time."

"That's great! Thank you, Carol, for your good effort. I shall look forward to seeing all of you tonight."

"Thank you, Mr. President", and she hung up.

Miles finished out the rest of his busy day. There were many, many things that required his attention and signature. His time was no longer his own, others directed his affairs. But he loved the power, the pomp and the glory. He was on top and it was great!

He thought about Ms. Carol Lumbro, who was in every way a beautiful woman, and when he looked at her he was moved by her. The beautiful shape of her gorgeous body. Oh! how he would love to take her to his lonely bed at night, but he must disregard that desire; there were just too many things that were more important.

At 5:00 p.m. sharp his door opened and two armed guards ushered him out to his waiting limousine. He was driven to the hotel and ushered up to his room. As the door closed behind him the phone rang. "Is what you have on the menu still okay for dinner this evening,

Mr. President?" This was his routine five days a week.

Miles took his bath, shaved, and slipped into a very lovely and comfortable robe. His dinner arrived, so he sat and ate. He wondered what Mr. Mirandola would be like. Carol had said he would be picked up at 7:00 p.m., so he had to get dressed; he was never late. In fact, he was always sitting, waiting with his hands folded when they came for him.

Miles, with his staff and six security people, arrived at a building in Lincoln Center. It was an extremely large concert hall. He and his staff were ushered to the front and seated in a very plush section, reserved for the elite. The place was packed and the curtains were drawn across a large stage. The lighting was somewhat dim and there was a constant roar of voices from the large crowd.

Miles sat looking around, he was concerned about what they were going to be watching. At that point in time he was uncertain about things. All that had happened made him question, down deep in his soul he wondered what was going on. What was his world coming to, could he really propagate his ideas or would there be further interference from outside his realm of understanding? His thoughts were interrupted as a very large man appeared from behind the curtains, dressed in a long black robe. The spot lights were turned upon him, as he began in a loud and clear voice, "Ladies and Gentlemen, may I present to you the greatest magician on earth, the great, the one and only, Mirandola!"

As the curtain opened, Mr. Mirandola, dressed in a long black robe, with a cane, and a funny looking top hat on his head, was standing beside a large table . Standing behind him were four assistants. Mr. Mirandola bowed, tipped his hat, and as he straighten he threw the cane to the floor. There was a puff of smoke with a noise, the cane disappeared, and a large python snake, about six feet long appeared. He reached down and took the thing just behind the head, lifted it over his shoulder, and it started to coil around him. He took off his hat, bowed and made a side-stepping move. There was another puff of smoke, and the snake disappeared; but sitting beside him on the table was a large striped tiger, sitting very calmly, with a leash about its neck. He reached and picked up the leash and patted the animal on the head. He stepped to one side and waved with his hand. Again there was a puff of smoke with noise. When it cleared, there he stood with the cane in his hand, the tiger and his top hat were gone. He bowed and the crowd went wild, with a very loud applause.

Miles wondered, how in the world did he do that? This was the most amazing thing he had ever seen.

Mr. Mirandola called out, "May we have some lady from the audience to assist in this next act?" One stood up from the audience, about 5'7", about 125 lbs., very shapely and beautiful. She was dressed in a nice, neat brown pant-suit. She walked very gracefully upon the stage, as everyone sat on the edge of their seats watching very calmly.

Mr. Mirandola had his assistants move the table slightly and cover it with a sheet and a pillow. Then he instructed the lady to get upon the table and lay flat on her back. Very gracefully she lay back upon the table, closed her eyes and folded her hands across her mid section. Mr. Mirandola waved his cane and there was a puff of smoke. When the smoke cleared, the lady was suspended about a foot above the table. He asked that the table be moved back, then the lady was suspended on her back in mid-air. He waved his cane and she began to float across the stage, still suspended in mid air. It appeared as if he was controlling her by remote control with his cane. He raised the cane and she raised to a height of about twelve feet, then he slowly pointed the cane toward the rear of the hall and she floated in the air toward the rear. As he would move the cane, she would move. He moved her all over, from wall to wall, up high, then he would bring her down just above the heads of the crowd, as if he was flying a model airplane. Finally he brought her back to the stage and lowered her back on the table. He made a downward motion with the cane and she sat up, turned around, moved off the table, bowed and left the stage.

For two hours Mr. Mirandola continued to perform, one thing after the other, it was mind boggling. Miles was amazed; he was convinced Mr. Mirandola had supernatural power, and that was great; he needed him to combat the old Prophet.

After the performance, they all returned to Miles' office. Ms. Lumbro brought Mr. Mirandola with her. As they settled in around the conference table, she took Mr. Mirandola around the table and introduced him to Miles and the entire group one by one.

After all the rituals, greetings and small talk subsided, Mr. Mirandola spoke up, "How can I be of service, Mr. President?"

Miles began, "We have a growing problem; it started in Jerusalem. There is a large, a very large group of Fundamentalist, who are creating all kinds of problems. Everything we here in the U.N. are trying to do, they oppose, especially our program of placing bar-coding on all our citizens. They are led by two old men who call themselves Prophets. They portray strange phenomenal power, and they contend it is a sign from God. We need to fight this fire with fire. When they speak and portray some strange thing, we want to speak and do something that will counteract what they do. Just enough to discredit what they are propagating. When we can get the laws set in place and the cooperation we need, they will be sent to prison for treason and that way we will eliminate them."

"I understand, Mr. President, and I think I can handle that", Mr. Mirandola spoke in a very enthusiastic manner. "You see, I also am endowed with strange phenomenal powers, some that I don't understand. But it works in conjunction with my mind, and I'm willing to do whatever I can to be helpful."

"Thank you, sir, I was impressed by what I saw tonight. There will be times when I'll need you to stand by my side. You and I will plan a trip to Jerusalem, before very long. I want to go there and see for myself what is going on."

"Yes, by all means, any way I can be helpful. I can cancel all my engagements and devote all my time to you and this Government."

"That will be wonderful, Mr. Mirandola. As of now, consider yourself employed by this Government as a staff person, with an allocation of one and one half times the amount you made last year. My secretary will be in touch with you for the arrangements . . . no, better still, Ms. Lumbro, will you take charge of this matter and make sure all is carried through to the satisfaction of Mr. Mirandola?

"Yes, I will be happy to do that, Mr. President. I'll see that he has an office here in this facility."

"Great! Mr. Mirandola, welcome aboard. Anything you need, let it be known." With that, Miles stood, and said, "My fellow workers, I believe that's all we have for tonight." Each one stood with him and said, "Good night, and thank you, Mr. President."

Miles sat there a long time after they all left, he felt elated. Just maybe I've found a way to offset the teachings of those old men, he thought.

THE TEN NATIONS

8

Places of registration were set up in every nation all over the earth. A large percentage of the people came in and registered eagerly. Only a few, by comparison, of the overall citizenship, refused to register. The general elections were held and ratified the nominations made by Miles and the Representatives.

The ten nations, also known as The Ten leading representatives and advisers to the President were: United States, Great Britain, France, Germany, Italy, Japan, Canada, Russia, China and Israel. These advisors were in direct contact with Miles.

Miles was elected President, Commander and Chief of all armed forces of the United Nations. He was given freedom of movement and could call for a military strike against a rebellious, disgruntled nation, if he considered it necessary for the good of the overall, without authorization of The Ten. He was placed in a very powerful position, but only if there was cooperation on the part of the existing nations, especially the United States.

It was proposed that each and every nation be phased out, that everything and everyone come under control of the United Nations. That was the intent, but it was a lot more easily said than done. When the transition started, there were divisions within the U.N. Some of the smaller nations did not want to cooperate and dissolve their government, nor their weapons systems, nor did they want to accept the universal monetary system, nor the universal language, nor the bar-code inventory. Miles was frustrated and disgusted with them. Many people were turning, and believing the old Prophet, as Cardinal Spilham had.

Miles established a daily TV program from the U.N., and he used Mr. Mirandola to portray many of his sorceries. Many were confused by that; it was a time of division, insomuch that Miles knew the use of force was inevitable. He would have to use force in order to bring about his vision for the world. He had the full cooperation and support from Mr. Davis and the United States, therefore he knew he could use overwhelming military power, but he was reluctant to take such drastic action. He did not know what to think about others of The Ten.

The old Prophets would stand every day, after the Evening Oblation of the Jews, and teach the Bible to the entire watching world. The large Prophet seemed to be the principle speaker, and he was a lot more agressive that the other. He would say, I'm fulfilling to the letter what Jesus said,-in Matthew-24:14-*And this gospel of the kingdom shall be preached in all the world for a witness unto all nations; and then shall the end come.*"

Miles tried in vain to have the Prophets cut off, and locked up, but people were afraid of them. Many people were uncertain about what the truth really was and therefore, Miles was not able to muster the support he needed.

Finally, after two years of strife and accomplishing very little, Miles grew desperate. He called his staff, and the ten leading representatives together around the conference table of his office. The ten representative were: Mr. Davis of the United States, Mrs. Majors of Great Britain, Mr. Filteau of France, Mr. Wilham of Germany, Mr. Musick of Italy, Mr. Ishikawa of Japan, Mr. Hampton of Canada, Mr. Tipliski of Russia, Mr. Chinn of China and Mrs. Rubin of Israel.

He sat in his chair looking fed up with them; there had been so much bickering back and forth. Some of them were willing to bring their governments into United Nations, change the momentary system, and be a real part of the new government. China and France were bitter against it. Israel and Russia were straddling the fence. They were so divided, every time an issue would come to the floor, they would bicker back and forth, and most of the time it was hard to pass any kind of a program.

Miles had tried appeasement, he had tried coercion, made many promises, but still they were hopelessly dead locked.

Miles sat and studied them a long time before he called them to order. He wondered about each of them; what were they thinking? Were they really being honest, or were they there because of the pressure and the prestige of their office? As he looked at each of them he wondered, did they believe him, or were some of them turning to the old Prophet? He wondered what they would be like, if each of them were in his position. He wondered why he was put in the situation he was in. They all sat for a long time and the chatter went back and forth. Miles sat there quietly, finally He spoke, his voice was stern and hard, his eyes were like fire. "May I have your attention, please. I want you all to know I've tolerated this bickering back and forth for two years. Not very much has been accomplished. We have sat on our own self interest, and our world has come apart. Instead of coming together as we should have, we have drifted every man in his own direction. That has to stop; we must get on with the business of building a better world, as we were elected to do."

"The trouble in Jerusalem has grown to the extent that the whole world is poisoned with that fundamentalist doctrine. I have reached the end of my tolerance and if it takes force to bring the nations into agreement, then force it will be . . . I serve you notice now; I will blow the opposition out of existence. I repeat to you, if . . . it is peace and cooperation by force, then, by force it will be! Do I make myself clear? HELLO! am I getting through to you?"

"I'm personally going to call the roster this morning, and I want each of you to answer me and tell me at this juncture what you intend to do. Do we come together as one, or must we be forced to come together? I'm thinking of the effect on the overall; no one of us is an island. What each of us do has a consequence on the entire world. Folks, it's either all or nothing, I believe we either do or we die, its just that simple."

"Mr. Davis for the United States, how do you and your government stand?"

"The United States is ready to put everything and everyone under control of the government of United Nations.

"Mrs. Majors for Great Britain, how do you and your government stand?"

"Great Britain is also ready to put everything and everyone under control of the United Nations."

"Mr. Filteau for France, how do you and your government stand?"

"France will not relinquish her government."

"The hell you wont! I told you . . . the time of tolerance is over. You have 72 hours to evacuate Paris. After 72 hours, I'll wipe Paris off the face of the earth! . . . I want you to understand . . . Mr. Filteau, France has hindered this organization long enough. Now . . . if you do not surrender your Army, with all its weapons, and pledge allegiance to the United Nations within 72 hours, Paris will be no more. I can assure you, that will only be the beginning. Instead of a nation that hinders, you will be a land of desolation and scorched earth within a few days. One way or the other, there will be no more France . . . Do I make myself clear?"

"Yes, Mr. President, I shall convey your message to my nation." he arose very upset, and left the room.

"Mr. Wilham for Germany, how do you and your government stand?"

"We of Germany are also ready to put everything and everyone under control of the United Nations."

"Mr. Musick for Italy, how do you and your government stand?"

"We of Italy are also ready to put everything and everyone under the United Nations."

"Mr. Ishikawa for Japan, how do you and your government stand?"

"We of Japan are also ready to put everything and everyone under the United Nations."

"Mr. Hampton for Canada, how do you and your government stand?"

"We of Canada are also ready to put everything and everyone under the United Nations."

"Mr. Tipliski for Russia, how do you and your government stand?"

"We of Russia are also ready to put everything and everyone under the control of United Nations."

"Mr. Chinn for China, how do you and your government stand?"

"We of China stand with you, Mr. President."

Miles noticed he did not say China was ready to put control of her government and weapons system under the United Nations. He wondered, should he take action or just let it ride. He sat and looked at Mr. Chinn and wondered, what would this great nation eventually do?

"Mrs. Rubin for Israel, how do you and your government stand?'

"We of Israel stand ready to relinquish control of our government, and place ourselves in the hands of the United Nations."

"Very good . . . now here is what I want to see happen; I want every soul alive registered. If they refuse to register, I want them put in prison. In prison we can care for them, but we must have a trouble free society.

The registration questionnaire shall consist of the following: Age, sex, height, weight, married or unmarried, children, place of birth, father and mother's names, and places of birth; names of brothers and sisters;— income, assets and religious persuasion. With the bar-code, the mark of inventory can be placed in the palm of the hand, or on the forehead if there is no hand. After the registration is complete, we will change the monetary system; we will be able to allocate to everyone, everywhere according to their need. Now, let's get cracking; time is of essence. Work together, no more bickering! My staff and I will assist in every way we can. I hope all of you understand me, we are now where the rubber meets the road, and there will be no more tolerance."

They all answered at the same time, "Yes, Mr. President."

Mr. Filteau entered the room and said, "Mr. President, France will cooperate in every way. We are ready to put all of France, with everyone and everybody under control of the United Nations."

"Thanks, Mr. Filteau, I'm glad. I'm reluctant to use the awesome power we have assembled, but let there be no mistake, I will if I have to."

"I plan to take Mr. Mirandola and Mrs. Rubin of Israel, and some of my staff, and go to Jerusalem in a few days. I want to personally look into the situation of the old Prophet. I want to thank all of you in advance for your cooperation. You are dismissed. Let's go to work."

They each stood and left with, "Thank you, Mr. President."

Miles sat there, he had a strange feeling about China. But he was determined to see the system working and on line. He would do what had to be done; Miles was that way, he knew where he was headed, and what he was trying to do.

9 DESTRUCTIN OF IRAQ

As another busy and frustrating year went flying by, it was filled with many hang ups, and no small amount of trouble. People were willing to register, but the Mark in their hand was something else. There were riots, marches and demonstrations. There were not enough police and jails to handle the opposition.

Miles thought within himself, I'm really going to have to get tough. Either people will take the mark, or else they will be put to death. There is just too much at stake, the very existence of mankind is weighed in the balances.

He called The Ten together, and sat at the head of the table looking at them. He had a habit of sitting and just looking at each one of them before he called them to order. His countenance was strong and he would stare hard at each one as if he was trying to read their minds. As he would look, they would notice him and drop their heads, as if it was hard to return his stare. Miles believed he made them feel uncomfortable. He wondered if they believed the strain of the office was having an effect on him. But he knew what he was doing, he truly believed he had to bring the world together before something very bad happened. He just did not believe for the most part they were all doing their best to bring it about.

Miles wondered just how many of them would stand with him if push came to shove. After a long time he

spoke, "May I have your attention, please. I've called
you in because I believe the time has come to take extreme action against the ones who are hindering our
system. You may ask me, how drastic? Well, I believe
we must begin putting people to death that take a stand
against the system. I have thought this through, and I
realize we can no longer coexist with the opposition.
I'm prepared to take the consequences if there are any.
I make a motion that we propose a law, and let it read
as follows: 'If a person refuses to receive the Mark, that
person will be put to death.' I know this is final, and extreme, and in as much as it is, I believe if we pass it, it
should be ratified by all nations and not just the Ten."

"Mr. President, I totally agree with you. We have tolerated all this balking and insurrection too long. It is
high time to take excessive action." Mrs. Majors spoke
very boldly.

Miles looked each of them in the eyes, and as he
would look, their would be a nod, insomuch that he
knew they would go along with him regardless how
they really believed.

The wording went out for ratification with a threat,
'Any nation who fails to support this law, will be destroyed.'

When the ballots came back, Iraq had voted it down,
all others had ratified it. Saddam Hussein's descendants
had been well trained and their arrogance was still evident.

Miles was very angry with Iraq after he saw the results. That one nation had caused so much trouble and
strife over the last few years! He sat and pondered, what
should he do? He said within himself, There is only one
answer, I must make an example out of them for the
good of all. He walked to his inter-office phone and
called his secretary, Ms. Price.

She answered very politely, "Yes, Mr. President?"

"Have Mr. Hussein, the Representative from Iraq, come into this office. You come in with him."

"Yes Sir," and she closed the circuit.

In a few minutes she and Mr. Hussein entered.

Miles sat in his plush chair and looked at Mr. Hussein a long time before he spoke. He was so sickened with him and with Iraq, when he did speak, he said, "Mr. Hussein, I know you are a cousin to Saddam, and all of you for a long time have been mavericks. I want you to send a message to the government of Iraq, let it read as follows: 'You have 72 hours to evacuate Bagdad; after that, your capital city will be destroyed.'— "Mr. Hussein, do you understand me? I intend to bring our world together, make no mistake about it, and I will do whatever it takes to get it done."

"You cannot do this Sir, the world will not stand still for this. We have our human rights."

"You *have* 72 hours, that's all! Get out of here! Go to work on your people, I've had all the disagreement from that country, and you I will tolerate."

Mr. Hussein sent the message, but Iraq made no reply; they really did not believe Miles would do anything as drastic as total destruction of a city.

After the 72 hours expired, Miles called Ms. Price, "Get me the Supreme Commander of the Navy."

"Yes Sir, right away, Sir."

Miles sat pondering the action he was about to take. He thought within himself, This is a drastic measure, and he wondered, Is this really justified? His thoughts were interrupted by the voice over the office system. "I have Admiral Bates on the line, Sir."

Miles picked up his phone and said, "Admiral Bates, I want you to order the Navy to hit Bagdad with Trident missiles, with hydrogen warheads The entire city must be destroyed in a flash. The time of rebellion, revolt, belligerence and insurrection is past, do I make myself clear?"

"Yes Sir, Mr. President, it will be done."

The order went out and without warning, and with pinpoint accuracy, the Navy hit Bagdad with hydrogen warheads from a Trident missile. The entire city was destroyed in a flash, thousands upon thousands of unsuspecting souls died. It was horrifying, only a few of the city were left alive, it made the atrocities of Adolf Hitler look small by comparison. Never in the history of man had an entire city been so completely wiped off the face of the earth by man, and it happened in a flash with no mercy whatsoever.

When Miles saw the report on the TV, he called Ms. Price again. "Get me the chief of the New York police on the line please."

It was only a couple of minutes and her voice came over the inter office system, "I have the chief on the line, Sir, go ahead.

Miles spoke very sternly, "Chief, I want you to arrest Mr. Hussein the Representative from Iraq. I want you to take him out and hang him from the overpass of a busy freeway. I'm going to get the attention of all the world, and they will know this government will do what it takes to bring our world together."

"Yes Sir, Mr. President, but shouldn't you give such an order as this to me in writing."

"Hell no! I want the whole world to know I'm in charge. When I give you an order I want it carried out, do you understand, Chief?" Miles was angry with him, and he knew it.

"Yes, Mr. President, it will be done."

The pictures of the missile and the hanging went out for all the world to see, the world realized Miles meant business He was getting tough; he had the power and was using it. The placement of bar-coding went into high gear. People everywhere and in everything, except the followers of Christ, were afraid for their lives. Miles was feared and that caused people to conform for the most part all over the world.

10 MILES IN JERUSALEM

On the first Monday morning after his action against Iraq, Miles summoned his staff and the ten people representing the top ten nations to his office. He sat in his chair and listened to the chatter back and forth. Everyone seemed to be in a good mood, and he had wondered how they would react after his drastic action against Iraq. He knew he had shown to the entire world he was getting tough. He wondered if they understood his motive, or were they now going along with him out of fear?

Finally he spoke, "Ladies and gentlemen, I think it is time for me to go to Jerusalem. I believe in that place lies the key to a lot of the rebellion that we are witnessing against our system. I think you all realize how vulnerable we are to this invasion force from outside our realm, and I believe we must be united in order to move forward to develop our defense against whatever it is. I realize our action against Iraq was extreme, but the only way I know at this point, is no longer to ask, but the time has come to demand what needs to be done."

"With the approval of this assembly I would like to have my private secretary, Ms. Price, with Ms. Lumbro, Mr. Mirandola, Mrs. Rubin, the representative from Israel, and several other staff people accompany me to the Middle East. We will go and take a first hand look at the things that are happening there, that seemingly have caused so much trouble. I would like to leave one week from today. Mr. Davis, you will act in my stead here while we are gone. I would like for you to consult with me before any major decision is made. What do all of you think?"

Mr Hampton of Canada spoke, "I think it is a great idea, perhaps if you are there in person you can stop some of the action from the fundamentalist who are seemingly at the heart of all the trouble. I personally am concerned about the old Prophets; I truly wonder where they came from. Until they appeared there on the steps of the temple, no one had heard of them. I's my conviction they are aliens left here by some U.F.O. creatures.

"I also, truly wonder", said Miles, "Do I hear a motion?"

Mr.Chinn of China, said,"I make the motion that you do that, Mr. President."

"All who favor, let it be known by raising your hand."

Every hand around the table went up at the same time.

Miles believed he still had the support of this body. After his drastic action, he wondered, but had hoped they would support him. He truly believed what he was doing was right.

Miles said, "Ms. Price, will you and Ms. Lumbro make all the arrangements?"

They both answered simultaneously, "Yes, Mr. President, we will get it done."

The following Monday morning, Miles, and his 20-member party boarded Air Force III and flew nonstop to Jerusalem.

During the flight, Miles' mind was working overtime. He was not sure how he would deal with the old Prophets. But he had known that sooner or later there would be a face to face showdown. He had the world's power behind him, and he truly wondered if it would be effective against the old men. He knew he would soon find out, this will be a make or break situation, he thought.

As the large jet circled the field at Jerusalem, Miles could see on the ground, a large crowd gathered. He remembered his first meeting with Mr. Davis and the Mayor of New York. Miles loved to fly, and as the large jet settled in, he was thrilled beyond words.

When they landed, the red carpet was rolled out, and a large band was playing; he did not know what, but it sounded great. As he walked down the steps, the large crowd began to cheer and applaud. At the bottom of the steps there was a microphone on a stand, and standing behind it was a man in a nice business suit and a M/Sgt. holding a golden key. As Miles approached the microphone, the band stopped and the man in the suit extended his hand and said, "I'm David Salman, Prime Minister of Israel. Welcome to the city of Jerusalem", and he gave the Sergeant a nod. The M/Sgt. stepped forward and said, "May we present to you the key to our city; welcome, Sir." He handed Miles the key and then took three quick steps backward and saluted Miles. The band started playing the Israeli anthem, and to Miles it seemed so slow. The music softened as the Prime Minister stepped to Miles' side and faced the crowd. "Friends and fellow citizens, may I present to you his Grace and now President of our United Nations, President Miles Abraham. By blood, he's one of our very own."

The Band stopped and Miles moved close to the microphone. He spoke in a very clear voice, "Mr. Prime Minister, fellow citizens we are delighted to be here. I've looked forward to a visit to this city for a long time. In fact, from the time I was a little boy, I've wanted to visit this famous city. I'm here today because I'm troubled over the many things that are negative toward our government. I'm hopeful that we can come to some common understanding and try to build instead of destroying. One of the first things on my agenda is, I would love to visit the Jewish Temple. I want to see first hand, the things that are being done there that are causing so much discord in our system of government. I would love to go stand on the steps, and from there, I shall speak to the world. But I serve notice now, we are determined to implement our system of government and any more dissension will have grave consequences. We are in a race with time; never has there been a more critical time in all the history of man. Our very existence depends upon our working together and developing ourselves, so friends, make no mistake, I intend to put a stop to the things that hinder."

When all the fan-fare was over and things settled down, Miles and his entourage were taken to Jerusalem's very finest hotel, and settled in.

The Prime Minister said, "Mr. President, anything you need, let it be known, this city is yours."

"As I said in my remarks, I would love to go visit the Jewish Temple."

"As you wish, Mr. President, we will make arrangements tomorrow. What time would you like?"

"Let's go tomorrow evening about sundown, I want to observe the things that are happening there at that time."

The motorcade was accompanied by armored cars and trucks with at least one hundred soldiers. They arrived just as the Jews were preparing to offer the Evening Oblation. Miles stood in the crowd of thousands, surrounded by guards and soldiers, watching. He became sickened with what he saw; he stepped forward, took a microphone of the sound system, and moved upon the steps of the Temple and stood there, without saying a word. He looked hard at the thousands and all things came to a halt, as very eye was focused upon him.

He began in a very loud, stern and angry voice, "I want this nonsense to stop. All this filth of killing lambs and burning them on this alter, is a stench in the nostrils of this great city. This is not a productive practice You people are wasting a lot of time, and hurting a cause that is trying to create a better world for you."

The Prophets appeared, making their way through the crowd of soldiers and guards that surrounded Miles. They moved onto the steps and came face to face with Miles. The entire world was watching and listening; this was their first meeting. They stood there looking at each other, the Prophets in their wrinkled and tattered clothes, Miles, in all his finery.

Miles had never seen anyone look so stern in all his life. The large Prophet's eyes were hard, and he looked straight at Miles, his countenance was that of contempt, and very stern! There was real boldness as he said, "My man . . . you . . . this day, have fulfilled what God said through Daniel a long time ago; before you and I were born. In Daniel 10:27-Daniel said, You, *shall cause the sacrifice and the oblation to cease, and for the overspreading of abominations you shall make it desolate.*"

"You have done precisely, what God said you would do. Your blindness is a mystery to me. I am reminded of the words spoken a long time ago by Paul in Acts-13:40-41-*Beware therefore, lest that come upon you, which is spoken of in the prophets; Behold, ye despisers, and wonder, and perish: for I work a work in your days, a work which ye shall in no wise believe, though a man declare it unto you.*"

"I declare unto you this day, you have desecrated this Temple. Your very presence is an offence to Almighty God . . . YOU AND YOUR IMMEDIATE PARTY SHALL BE SMITTEN WITH BLINDNESS FOR SEVEN DAYS!" They turned abruptly and left.

Miles, Ms. Price, Ms. Lumbro, Mr. Mirandola and Mrs. Rubin were immediately stricken with total blindness. It was so dark, and such a awesome feeling within Miles! He had never felt so humiliated in all his life. Here he was the most powerful man on earth, and now he was stumbling around feeling for someone to take him by the hand and lead him away. Miles wondered if the old man had released some kind of poison gas. This guy had to be from another realm, and he swore within himself he would stop him, even if he had to kill him. He was not going to disrupt things any longer, this trick was the final straw.

Miles and his party were taken back to the hotel and at Miles request were locked in behind closed doors with guards posted out side each door to assure no intrusion. Miles did not want any of them to be seen, nor did he want to talk to anyone. The only contact he would allow with the out side world was when they brought him his food.

Miles could feel his way around in his rooms somewhat, but there were times when he could not tell where he was; he would stumble and fall. He could bathe and dress himself. He did not try to shave. It was the worse time of his life. He slept most of the time. There was no TV, only sound and that was frustrating. When he was awake, he just sat and stared at the blankness. When he ate, he would drop his food and spill his drinks. He had never realized just how awful it was to be blind. He had to learn to do all things by feel and that took some doing. He would not take telephone calls, as far as he was concerned his world came to an abrupt standstill when the blindness came.

After seven days of that frustration and torment, all their eyesight came back as strangely as it had gone. As soon as he could see again, Miles was extremely angry. I will learn what that old man is all about, or I will die trying, he thought.

Miles called the Prime Minister. "Mr. Salman, I want to return to the Temple in the same fashion, and at the same time as the other day."

"As you wish, Mr. President. Are you sure you want to have anything to do with that old guy? You know he called down fire on some of our people. He has something none of us understand, and frankly I'm afraid of him. We have elected as much as possible, to leave him alone."

"Yes, you have left him alone, and he has poisoned the minds of thousands. I've tolerated him long enough; I'm going to put a stop to this, whatever it is he has. I truly believe this is an invasion from outer space, and if it is, we have to get to the bottom of it. Just make sure your soldiers are loaded with live ammunition. We will see how he handles bullets."

"Mr. President, as you wish, we are with you all the way", The Prime Minister answered, trembling. Not only was he afraid of Miles, he was also afraid of the old prophets.

Miles and his motorcade, with better than one hundred soldiers arrived at the Temple just at sundown. Miles walked to the steps surrounded by guards and soldiers, and took the microphone. The lights and cameras were turned on as he spoke. "Citizens of the world, I do not understand this strange phenomenal power this old man has, but I'm here this evening to put a stop to the things being propagated from this hallowed place."

The two old Prophets appeared, and moved up on the steps. Miles let them get close to him, then he said,

"SHOOT THEM . . . we will see who has power with God!"

Several shots rang out, and the two old prophets, without a word, dropped dead on the spot.

Miles stood there looking down at them. Blood was coming out of them, pouring down the steps, as they quivered and died.

Miles was confused, they died like any other human being. Their blood looked human just like anyone else.

A man stepped out of the crowd and said, loud and clear, "My man you have fulfilled to the letter what John wrote to the Churches two thousand years ago, in The Revelation 11:7-10-*And when they shall have finished their testimony, the beast* (system) *that ascendeth out of the bottomless pit shall make war against them, and shall overcome them, and kill them. And their dead bodies shall lie in the street of the great city, which spiritually is called Sodom and Egypt, where also our Lord was crucified. And they of the people and kindreds and tongues and nations shall "see" their dead bodies three days and an half, and shall not suffer their dead bodies to be put in graves. And they that dwell upon the earth shall rejoice over them, and make merry, and shall send gifts one to another; because these two prophets tormented them that dwelt on the earth.*"

Miles looked at him in disgust and said, "Shoot him, also!" The rifles cracked and the man fell dead beside the two prophets.

The camera zoomed in upon them, so all could have a close look; the entire world was watching. Another man stepped forward and said, "Mr. Smart Man, you do not realize you've just fulfilled one of the great things spoken of, by our Lord. A short time ago, this prophecy of the entire earth being able to look upon a scene in the streets of Jerusalem, was thought to be ridiculous, and certainly unbelievably. But with the development of TV, and the Satellite Transfer System this is now possible."

Miles shouted, "SHOOT HIM ALSO!"

Again the rifles cracked and that unknown man dropped dead also. Miles took the microphone again and said, "I'm not proud of the fact that these had to be executed, but I must send a message. We have tolerated all this nonsense long enough. Our world is at stake, our very existence as earthly people is at risk. We cannot, and I mean in no way, can we permit further disloyalty. We must move forward and come together. We have the means to give to every citizen plenty, and soon I hope we will develop a system that can defend itself against an invasion from the unknown world. But the system must be implemented. I want the world to know it will be accomplished. We have wasted three and a half years with arguments back and forth." There was a loud cheer from the crowd, and people began to applaud. Miles knew there was still opposition, but he felt he was at last bringing it under control.

He continued very bold in his tone, "I want these two trouble makers left here for seven days. You can take the other two and bury them. But I want the world to look upon these two so called Prophets. Where is their power with God now? I want to send a message, we will fight every force that dares to disrupt our system and tries to destroy the unity we are trying to establish. I'll be the first to admit, a lot about these two I do not understand, but one thing is for sure, they will trouble us no more. The same thing shall apply to all the rest who oppose the new system; I can only hope I've sent the right message." Miles left the steps as the throng cheered. He could see there was overwhelming support for what he had done. He and his party were driven back to the hotel.

11 THE GREAT EARTHQUAKE

Back in the hotel, Miles turned the TV on. The pictures were coming live from the steps of the Temple. There was a re-run of the entire event of him having the Prophets shot. Then, a flash-back of the destruction of Iraq, and a re-play of Mr. Hussein hanging from the freeway overpass.

The commentator said, "Folks, our President means business. He will bring this world together, and as you can see, he's willing to use force to do it. I think he is to be praised; we of the world have procrastinated long enough. It is a mystery to me why people cannot see his point. In my judgment he is only trying to build a better, safer world. He certainly has this commentators support. Instead of so much contention and hindering, we should be working and pulling together."

The camera focused live on the two old Prophets, and the commentator was silent. They lay as they had fallen, on their backs with their heads laying down the steps and their faces could be plainly seen. Their bodies were riddled with bullets and the blood had soaked through their clothing. On-lookers were milling about; it was a very eerie sight and a strangeness hung over the night. The night air seemed black and silent. There was that empty, emotional feeling of death. It was sad to see them, their blood running down the steps had hardened, but was very visible.

The commentator broke the silence as he said, "Well,

I guess our President did what he knew needed to be done. These two have certainly hindered, and created a great following. Now we will see who has power with God, if there is a God as they contended. I wonder where He is now?"

Miles pushed the off-button on his remote and turned to other things. He had done what had to be done. He hated it, but the world system was more important to him than those two old trouble-makers. Moreover, he just was not sure where they came from; these were strange times. He had been tolerant, but he knew if he was to accomplish what he had set out to do, he had to bring it all under control, and in three and one half years very little had been done.

Two days went by. Every day at noon, and on the 6:00 p.m. news, the TV would focus upon the two old men. The commentator would come on and comment and ridicule what they stood for. Mail began to pour in from around the world, and there was overwhelming support for what Miles had done.

Miles' phone rang. He answered, "Hello, this is President Miles."

The operator, in a very pleasant voice said, "Mr. President, I have Mr. Davis from United Nations on the line."

"Please put him through."

Miles heard the click and then,"Hello, Mr. President, Doyle Davis here."

"Yes, hello Doyle, how are you?"

"I'm doing great Sir, everyone is pleased with what you did. Things are really beginning to come together. I thought you would be happy to hear, people are coming to the polling places in droves; the bar-coding is in full swing. Looks like we will have the system up and on-line a lot sooner than we thought. Thank you, Mr.

President, we are all grateful to you; you did what had to be done. Anything you want done, give me a call."

"Thanks, Doyle, I'm going to stay on here a few days. In fact, I've been thinking about establishing an office here. This city has always been a place seemingly dear to the heart of God. I stand as the representative of God, so it might be good if I was here, so people could come to me. I would like for us to give that some thought."

"Yes, Mr. President, we of United Nations stand solid with you."

"Thank you, Doyle, that's comforting to me, so long for now", and he hung up.

At noon on the fourth day, Miles was in his hotel suite. He turned his TV on to catch the noon news. The pictures were coming live from the steps of the Temple. The commentator was speaking, "Folks, I think our President's point is well taken; these guys are a good example, but they are really beginning to stink. The camera zoomed in on the two old men. They were black, bloated, with their mouths wide open, laying just as they had fallen, and flies were swarming all over them. It was a putrefying sight, sickening to look at even on TV. This picture was going out live all over the earth, and would be shown on tape again and again at different times. The camera turned to the commentator as he said, "These guys are beginning to get ripe . . . Wait a minute! . . . WHAT IS THIS?" The camera turned back to the two bodies, the flies were leaving, and the blackness began to turn white. Then they began to stir, and it could be seen they were coming back to life. "I . . . I . . . I'll . . . b... be... damned! . . . THESE GUYS ARE COMING BACK TO LIFE! . . . before my very eyes!"

As the entire world watched, including Miles, the

two Prophets stood up alive. Then they began to rise, and it looked as if they just floated up into heaven and out of sight. There was a shock wave that passed over the entire watching world. This really got their attention . . . the world was glued to the TV. Then there was a very loud sound; as if a thousand jets were passing over, and things began to shake.

Miles had a large round solid oak table in his room, with a large column as a center support for the four legs. He dove under the table and wrapped his legs and arms around the column. Everything shook, the table flew all over the room from wall to wall, then the ceiling came crashing in.

The earth shook and the sky shook. The Satellite Transmitting and Relay System, (acronym STARS) fell and hit the earth. Planes, cars and trains crashed. The great old buildings of Europe that withstood World War II fell flat. Every building, bridge, freeway, airport runway, parking garage, power line, pipe line, water dam, generating station, radio tower, transmitting dish, micro wave tower, telephone cable and railroad on earth were destroyed. Never had there been such a shaking in all of the recorded history of mankind. The shaking went on and on; it must have gone past ten on the Richter scale. Great ships and subs were turned upside down and sank in the shaking, raging water Great waves swept ashore and carried people and objects out and into the sea. All power went off, the magnetic field was thrown off; nothing electrical would work. No motor would run, no light would burn. When the shaking stopped, the wheels of mortal man . . . stood deathly still. The fires burned, the dust and smoke rose high into the sky. Although it was high noon in Jerusalem, it was dark. All communications were knocked out. There was no more radio, TV, nor telephone. The electronic spectrum was thrown completely off; no battery-powered equipment would work; everything was down. The entire earth staggered in gloom, chaos, astonishment, disorder, suffering, and death.

One moment the entire world was watching TV, looking upon the two old men, the next, everything went blank. All over the earth millions were instantly killed. There was not a spot on earth that did not shake.

There was not one believer in Christ left; all were taken out, and passed through the Valley of the Shadow of Death. It all lasted for a full five minutes.

When the shaking stopped and Miles regained his senses he realized he was not really hurt, just shaken up and bruised. As the dust cleared, he could see light, so he crawled out and onto what had been the street. He could hear the groans and the screams of the trapped, the wounded and dying. It was awful; fires raged, smoke and the stench of burning flesh were everywhere; never had there been anything like that. He wandered around in a daze. It seemed like a bad dream, unreal. Finally he got his bearing and made his way toward what was the City Hall. He came upon a group of people gathered together, one of them was the Prime Mister.

He saw Miles, "Thank God you are alive, Mr. President! Thank God, at least you are still with us. Damn, that was something else!'

"Yes, I'm not hurt, how can I help?"

The Prime Minister said, "Please, just sit here", as he pulled up a chair. "We will really need you to pull the people back together, once we get things straightened out," he sighed. It was almost a cry of despair. "We are trying to find medical supplies so a facility can be set up. I have a few soldiers and policemen who have reported in. They are out trying to round up whoever and whatever we can save and salvage. There is no water to fight the fires. All communications are out; things are bad Mr. President, but thank God, you are still alive."

Millions were burned to death, others were crushed and died a slow agonizing death under all that had fallen on them. For hours the groaning and crying of the trapped and dying could be heard. It was a time of trouble such as had never been before.

Miles sat there scared, with his hands folded in his lap wondering, his world was really coming apart. No way could he know the extent of the damage. He watched, as the people brought in things they were digging out. Doctors showed up, medical supplies were brought in, a hospital facility was set up and the wounded were treated. There was only voice communications. No motors would run, so everything had to be done and carried by hand. Water, when it could be found, was brought in by hand in buckets. Only canned food was left, the frozen soon began to spoil. They were trapped, just a small group, and Miles wondered what it was like over the other parts of the world. To what extent this catastrophe had happened, they had no way of knowing. Miles wondered if help would be arriving from the outside world. He did not realize what was wrong, nor why no electrical device whatsoever would work.

In a split second, the world where men could look upon each other and speak to each other from every square inch of the earth, regardless of position; it was now reduced to where men could only see and speak over a distance of a few yards.

A man from the Utility Commission came in and the Prime Minister said, "What can you tell us?

"Mr. Prime Minister, I don't understand it, but the magnetic field is no longer synchronized as it was, I guess, I really don't know. Nothing that is tied to the electronic spectrum will work. There is no way we can know how wide-spread this is; we are back to square one. Our world, that is this part of it, is changed and there is nothing we can do. We have no electricity whatsoever, and my man, that's bad! No computer, no TV, no telephone, no radio, no motor will run, nothing will work, and no electrical light will burn. We are dead in the water. Those of us who are alive will have to start from scratch and try to dig out."

Not only did it look bad to Miles, IT WAS BAD! The only shelter they had were the tents they were able to dig out and save.

Six days dragged by; there was no word from the outside world. Every once in a while there would be an aftershock. The city of Jerusalem was total destruction. Outside on the Mount of Olives, which had split, they could see a valley like a runway, running out across the wilderness as far as the eye could see.

On the sixth day Miles was sitting out side his tent. There was another rumbling, then it turned to a roar, and things started shaking again. Miles grabbed a large piece of steel, protruding out of a large hunk of concrete and hung on. Again, everything shook and shook, and people and things were thrown all over the place. When it settled down and finally stopped, alarms were sounding everywhere. That meant the earth's magnetic field had rocked back into synchronization and the electrical things would once again work. What a wonderful thought it was, as the alarm bells began to sound, and the battery powered devices once again came to life!

THE REBUILDING

12

Slowly things were dug out. Every day Miles sat in his chair outside his tent and watched what he could see. His entire staff were also spared and they were all given tents close to Miles. Portable toilets and showers were set up. An army style-kitchen was established and the Prime Minister made every effort to make them as comfortable as possible. Miles was under the guard of security agents and soldiers twenty four hours a day. When he went to the toilet or to the shower, the places were cleared first. His meals were served to him in his tent. He could sit out-side but the area around the compound was patrolled by soldiers out for 5,000 yards to make sure, he was kept safe.

Time dragged, one week then two, and they were into the third week when the Prime Minister said to Miles, "Mr. President, the communications people tell me we should be able to contact New York by radio in the morning."

"That would be great, Mr. Prime Minister. I would surely love to try and reach Mr. Davis, and try to learn what is left of the United Nations."

"Very well, Sir, we will try the first thing in the morning, say around 8:am, that way it will be around 5:pm there", the Prime Minister said, pleased he could have a little part in trying to bring things back together.

"Thank you, Mr. Prime Minister, for your good effort, you have certainly been helpful; I'll see you the first thing in the morning," Miles said. He was very grateful to the Prime Minister.

The next morning, Miles was ushered into the communications tent at 8:am. The operator motioned for him to sit in a chair, then He said, "This is Jerusalem calling New York,—over."

Through heavy static a voice came back. "This is New York, go ahead Jerusalem, I read you 5 by 5,—over."

" I have the President of United Nations here with me, and he would like to speak to a Mr. Davis, the speaker of the house at United Nations,—over."

Well, I'll declare, great minds do run in the same channel. He's here with me now, we were going to try and reach you about 9:am your time,—over."

"Great, please put him on,—over."

The operator handed the microphone to Miles and said, "Go ahead Sir."

Miles took the microphone and rather awkwardly pushed the button and said, "Doyle can you hear me?—over".

"Yes, Mr President I can hear you loud and clear,—over."

"How are things there, Doyle, are all of you still alive?—over"

"Yes, Mr. President, how about your staff?—over."

"We're all still alive, just battered, bruised and some are really shook up, but we're okay. They tell us it will be at least eight weeks before our plane and the conditions will be so we can return. Can you pull the pieces back together?—over."

Yes Sir, we have it under control and we'll look for you all in about eight weeks,— over.

"That's great, Doyle, I'm in a tent only a short distance away, so if you need me you can call me,—over."

"Do you have any special instructions, Mr. President?—over."

"Please try to get some kind of an estimate on how destructive that quake really was. Doyle, you are in control until I get back, do whatever has to be done. Use your own judgment and as I said, you can contact me if you need me, otherwise I'll see you in about eight weeks. So long for now,—out."

Miles was escorted back to his tent and left alone. He was greatly relieved to know Mr. Davis was still alive and in control. He knew in his mind, he could handle things. He entered his tent and started planning on how they were going to rebuild.

It took several weeks to get the airports opened, and the traffic control reestablished to where flights could resume. Miles and his staff were stranded in Jerusalem for two months after he talked to Mr. Davis, until planes were repaired, and oversees flights were resumed.

When Air Force III was finally put back in service, a new crew took over, and flew Miles and his group back to New York. They found Mr. Davis and his staff waiting at the Kennedy Air Terminal.

As Miles stepped off the plane, he saw Mr. Davis and part of his staff.

Mr. Davis ran to Miles and embraced him and said, "Oh! thank God you're alive, Mr. President, we're all so happy to see you. It has been a rough time."

"We're all okay now, just got stranded for a few days. How are things here, Doyle?"

"Everything has been destroyed, but we are set up in a makeshift fashion. We have large tents set up for the U.N. Your office was reestablished similar to the original, only in a tent. There's no telephone as yet, but we do have some portable radios."

"Mr. President, we have salvaged a lot of equipment,

and have it in tents. Emergency generators are set up, and things are working, some-what. We have real trouble with the waste and water systems. Things are still rather out of control. When it was realized that all systems were down, people turned animalistic, and practically over-night the world turned into a dog-eat-dog situation. The ones with guns took from others what they wanted. There were killings, rapes and wholesale robbery. People just went wild and took what they could, until the armies could be reassembled to bring some order. I took charge and declared marshal law. I ordered the looters, murderers and rapists shot on the spot. I've had tapes of the order flown to every part of the world we're able to reach at this time. We have ordered that they be shown on each new local TV station, as it is restored. That action, I hope, will settle things down somewhat. When people realize there's still a government in charge, maybe they will quieten down."

"A very limited amount of air traffic control is being put into service. TV is established in a limited fashion. When we're able, tapes will have to be flown throughout the world and aired on local TV stations. By this method I believe we can bring the world back together. We have already started printing a new currency. That can be flown and distributed throughout the world. The data on the bar-code system is now either destroyed or useless. We will have to start over and build back."

"Doyle, how many of The Ten representatives are accounted for?"

"All of them sir, now that Mrs. Rubin is back with you."

"That's great! Call a meeting of The Ten in my office tomorrow morning. We'll move forward. Time is of the essence. But Doyle, before you go, I want to thank you for the wonderful way you have handled things."

"I was only doing my job, Mr. President; thank God, you're still with us."

Miles' quarters was a large tent, but they had everything he needed to make his life comfortable. Guards and soldiers were posted around the tent.

The next morning at precisely 9:30 a.m., Miles was ushered into his office. The Ten and his staff had gathered. He settled into his chair at the head of the table and said, "It's wonderful to be back with you. This has been a terrible time. But let's not be discouraged, we can build back."

Mr. Chinn from China spoke up, "Mr President, we of China no longer desire to be a part of the U.N. Our people want to maintain their own government. On behalf of the Government of China, we respectfully withdraw. If you want to take offence and go to war with us, we are ready for that. But let me warn you, with the great first-strike potential gone; I do not think you can win a war with China."

Miles knew he was right, in fact he wondered what kind of a fighting force they had left. He knew he had to have time to rebuild the defense systems and at this time he had no idea what was involved. Miles sat there and looked at him a long time and he noticed Mr. Chinn glared back at him. Miles could feel the hate in the man and he knew there was contempt for him personally. His mind was racing within him as he said, "How about the rest of you, how do you stand?"

Mr. Davis spoke up, "We're all still together. In just a few days we will have a common monetary system, with the new paper money. It will take time to recover the data in the bar-code system, but in time it will all straighten out. I truly believe we are a lot better off, if we work together."

Miles answered, "That's my conviction also. But if

China wants to withdraw, let it be. The worse thing we could do now is start a war among ourselves. We have the enormous task of rebuilding and reestablishing."

"Mr. Chinn, you are excused; inform your Government we will accept its withdrawal, thank you." Mr Chinn stood up and left without a word.

Miles knew with things in such disarray he did not dare rock the boat and challenge him. Instead, he said, "Do I hear a suggestion, we need a replacement for Mr. Chinn?"

Mr. Musick of Italy spoke up, "Mr. President, Mr. Montoia of Spain is a wonderful man. Spain has been helpful in every way, I suggest we nominate him."

"Is there a second?"

Mr. Tipliski said, "I second."

"All in favor, please raise your right hand." All hands went up.

Miles said, "He will be temporary, until a general election can be held."

"Ms. Lumbro, would you mind calling him in?"

"Yes I will, thank you, Mr. President"; she stood and gracefully left the room.

Miles continued, "We must put studies into motion to determine what is left that we can use, and the best way to go about it."

Again Mr. Davis spoke up, "Mr. President, I've already authorized a study by two leading companies in their fields. We have the experts in the outer office with a report."

"Thank you, Mr. Davis, could we have them called in?"

"Yes, Mr. President, Ms. Price, would you please call them in."

Two very distinguished gentlemen were ushered into the room and were given chairs at the conference table. Mr. Davis spoke, "May I introduce Mr. Keating from

Lockheed/Martin, and Mr. Cramer from Bechtal. These two men are leaders in each of their fields. Mr. Keating is one of the world's greatest authorities on space and space equipment, Satellites and such. Mr. Cramer is the most knowledgeable in general heavy construction. I have asked them to make a study, and give us a quick estimate on damage and time involved to restore."

"Mr. Keating, we will call you first."

"Thank you, Mr. Davis, in the little over seven weeks since you contacted me, we have found that all satellites are down. The facilities to build more were all destroyed. We are looking at least two years before another one could be launched. But we still have Aircraft that we can use to relay data; that will require some reprogramming, and retrofit, but it can be done. We can station them around the world, fly around the clock, and reestablish world-wide radio and possibly. TV communications. It seems almost miraculous but very little of the jet fuel, gasoline and oil supply were destroyed. The storage containers were built so strong most of them are still in tact. This gives us the much needed time to get the refineries back up and working again. Most of the coal and nuclear generators can be repaired rather rapidly. It wont take long to get the power distribution back up. We have large crews working day and night. Six months will make a lot of difference. Understand, it will be a make-shift thing, and certainly in no way will it reach the perfection we had. But we spent the better part of ninety years building the system that was destroyed in five minutes."

At that time, Ms. Limbro entered with Mr. Montoia.

"Mr. President, ladies and gentlemen, may I present to you, Mr. Montoia. I've explained to him the action of this group."

Mr. Mantoia spoke, "Thank you, Mr. President and

fellow citizens. I proudly accept your nomination."

"Thank you, Mr. Montoia, please take that seat there", and Mr. Davis pointed to the seat left vacant by Mr. Chinn.

Mr. Montoia sat, and from all around the table there was, "Welcome aboard, Mr. Montoia."

Mr. Davis spoke, "Thank you, Mr. Keating, for your report and for your suggestions. Mr. Cramer of Bechtal, what do you have to report?"

"Thank you, Mr. Davis. Our study revealed that all power and telephone lines are destroyed. The ones above ground were knocked down, and the ones below ground were all pulled apart. There was so much movement of the earth, the conduits below ground were destroyed. We will have to start from scratch and replace them, which will be very slow. All micro-wave relay towers and the cables leading to them were destroyed. All water, gas, drainage and sewer systems are destroyed. These can be rebuilt fairly fast, and city to city communications can be restored in a few months. In some cases it will be better for cities to relocate and start from scratch. All major freeways are closed. We will have to construct temporary roads until the permanent roadways can be restored."

"With the aircraft relays that Mr. Keating spoke of, radio communications can be established all over the world in a very short time. By all of us working together, we can be talking to each other, and living fairly normal lives world-wide again in a year or two."

"We still have all the heavy equipment in tact, the big earth movers and so forth. As fast as we dig it out it is put back in service, and already things are beginning to turn around."

"Thank you, Mr. Cramer," said Mr. Davis.

Miles spoke up, "I believe we would be wise to reestablish our facility for the United Nations in Jerusalem.

That city has always been a sacred place where people go to seek spiritual guidance. I believe we should be there. If you feel the U.N. could best be served here in New York, then we can rebuild the buildings here. What is your opinion?"

Mr. Davis said, "I believe you have a good idea, Mr. President. At this time it would be six of one, and half dozen of the other, to rebuild here, or in Jerusalem."

Mr. Cramer spoke, "I think it would be better to rebuild in Jerusalem. We'll be more effective over there, and it will be easier. This New York city is a mess and it's going to be hard to rebuild here on top of this ruin. There is another factor, Jerusalem has always been considered the center of the world."

Mr. Davis said, "Thank you, Mr. Cramer for that input. I believe you have a good point, Mr. President. We can load everything we have salvaged here, on C-5 transports and be set up there within four weeks. We can begin to rebuild from there. Jerusalem will then be the Capital of the United Nations."

More or less all together, the voices from the table echoed, "Sounds good to me."

Mr. Davis said, "Do I have a motion that we relocate to Jerusalem?"

Mr. Filteau, of France said, "Mr. Chairman, I make the motion that we move the Capital of the United Nations to Jerusalem, and start rebuilding there."

"All in favor, please raise your right hand."

Every hand in the room went up and Mr. Davis said, "So be it."

Miles spoke,"Shall we adjourn, and resume business in Jerusalem, in tents, four weeks from today? In the mean time Mr. Cramer and Mr. Keating, take charge of the reconstruction and pull out all stops. If money is needed we will print more money."

"I second that, Mr. President. I and my staff will personally attend to the details and see that it is done," Mr Davis spoke with a very positive note.

Miles said, "With the help of my staff, we will work on the internal affairs of the United Nations, and thanks to all of you in advance for your cooperation." With that, they all stood and filed out.

The work of relocating went into full swing. There was a spirit as of one man to rebuild. Every piece of equipment and every available person was put to work in the service of the United Nations, except China. China elected to rebuild their country on their own. Miles thought within himself, I will have to deal with China before very long. Oh, how he did wish the great Trident system was still functional, but he knew at this point it was not, and he had no idea how long it would take to evaluate and perhaps salvage some of it. He knew even if he could find some of the subs still in tact, it would take time to rebuild a guidance system, even using the planes as Mr. Keating had suggested. Well, he would take it one step at a time, but his spirit was not broken. He did not understand all that had happened, but he would use it to an advantage.

13 THE GRAET TRIBULATION

After four weeks, the U.N. was moved from New York City and established in Jerusalem. Miles had the Army force the Jews that were there trying to rebuild and reestablish their form of worship, completely out of the city of Jerusalem. He did not realize that he was fulfilling what was written of him almost twenty-seven hundred years before in Daniel 9:27- *And he shall confirm the covenant with many for one week:* (7-yrs.) *and in the midst of the week he shall cause the sacrifice and the oblation to cease, and for the overspreading of abominations he shall make it desolate, even until the consummation, and that determined.* There were no spiritual people left to rebuke him; God completely turned Miles over to Satan and to his reprobate mind.

From the U.N., under the direction of Mr. Keating and Mr. Cramer, the construction crews were formed and sent out with lightening like speed, and the rebuilding went into full swing. Miles had an army of construction workers pull out all stops and devote all their time to building a Temple for him. The wheels of restoration were set in motion all over the world. The manufacturing of goods, cars, trucks, tractors and heavy construction equipment forged ahead, even exceeding the way it was in WW II. Every one had a job and the government made sure they were rewarded for the labor. Everything that could be dug out, was salvaged and put back into use. New crops were planted and it looked as if things would turn around in a few short years. Tents by the millions, were manufactured and distributed for temporary shelter and housing. When more money was needed, the presses would roll and more was printed. There was a make-shift method of the distribution of money by air, and most of the people's needs were met. Things really moved forward for the first year after the big quake, and it seemed there was a wonderful spirit of cooperation all over the world, except for China.

The Ten were in session five days a week from 9:30 a.m. to 5:00 p.m. and the affairs of the world were handled smoothly. Within that first year; Miles miraculously had them complete the construction of the large Temple in Jerusalem on the old Temple sight. The new Temple was round, very large, and opened into the East. Large circular steps made up the approach; there were ten large double doors leading into the narthex with water falls and winding stairways leading up to the balconies, beautiful hanging light fixtures, decorations and statues of many descriptions. Much of what had been salvaged from the beautiful works of old, were on display. There were ten doors leading into the main floor, from aisles that went around on either side. The Temple had a seating capacity of approximately ten thousand. It had beautiful curved balconies, lovely soft cushioned seats in circle rows, stepped, so there was a view from every seat. The acoustics were perfect; the sound system and the lighting were variable, the best! It was plush! In the front was a large round stage that revolved. Large circular curtains opened and closed. Miles had them construct a pulpit on a hydraulic ram, so it would raise and lower. Miles would lecture there, and Mr. Mirandola would perform; scenes could be changed with ease. None of what was left of the Jewish nation was allowed to worship there, and certainly no

animal sacrifice was allowed. In fact, Miles went all out
to destroy that form of worship. He had a deep-rooted
hatred for that religion that stemmed from his youth
when he, as a child, was forced to participate.

Miles had the army of construction workers construct an office in the Temple, similar to the one he had
in New York. People under very rigid control, could
come to him there. Next to the Temple, he had them
construct a nice, large apartment for him and his staff.
This wonderful facility was completed, within eighteen
months after the starting date. That project was given
top priority, while other things, such as items for defense were neglected.

Three times a week Miles would lecture. The entire
programs were video-taped, flown and shown on local
TV all over the world. In that way, Miles was in touch
with the world, and the world was very much under his
control.

In his heart, Miles did not really believe in the existence of a God, intrinsically. He had gone into the Catholic Church because of what they had to offer him. He
wanted the power and the prestige the Church could
give. He worked hard, and kept what he really thought,
to himself. There was just too much to the universe; to
him it was absurd to believe there was a power great
enough to control everything. In his true way of thinking, all that could be seen and known about the macrocosm, with all the crashing, revolving, colliding,
exploding planets and galaxies, was too much. He believed man could see what had evolved, perhaps from
the Big Bang, billions of years ago, who knew? In his
heart, he believed in the evolution of all things including man. He truly believed there was life on other planets, and that the mysterious disappearance of people
four and a half years ago, was truly a visitation from
someone out there, further advanced. His dream was to

advance mankind in technology and science, so they also would be able to move into other dimensions, somewhere in outer space.

In the past he had preached and practiced religion because it was the thing to do in order to get where he wanted to be. As he increased in status, he found it acceptable to say and do things in the name of God, but he began to believe that man was God to himself, and within himself; therefore he was able to say, without conscience, that he in fact was God. He had risen to the place where he was one man, over the entirety of mankind on earth, with exception of China, and he could do all things that were humanly possible as he desired. Someone out there somewhere was trying to disrupt things for him, but he was like a bulldog; he would hang on and not give up.

He utterly ignored the Bible, with its Spiritual teachings. Really, to him it was all a lot of nonsense. All the prophecy, all the signs, symbols, the rituals and ceremonies, that in fact prophesied and portrayed the coming of Christ and the consummation of all things, went over his head. He did not realize that no mortal man can comprehend the great omnipotent eternal God, with His working in space and time. All that was far past Miles' understanding. He completely missed the fact that God had shown His existence through His Son who came into the world. All of that was absurdity to Miles.

He said things as if he believed in Jesus and the Virgin Mother, but in reality, it was all idle talk to him. But now, *He* was the all powerful one, and that made him God to the people. If anyone dared say otherwise, he had the power to eliminate them, and that is what he did. All opposition to him or the system, was put to death. Great fear of him moved over the entire world.

He would declare that he was God's representative

on earth. If people wanted to come to God, they would have to come through him. His saying that, made the churches mad, including his own Catholic church. War broke out among the churches. The Ten sent troops to put that down, and many of the leaders of the existing churches were killed. Over night, trouble erupted all over the earth.

After one year and six months passed from the great quake the atmospheric conditions suddenly changed. Some days it would be so hot men could not live outside and many that were in tents died from the heat. Great cumulonimbus clouds reaching up to 90,000 feet in the air would develop, then extreme lightening and thunder storms would follow, with high winds and tornados and great hail-stones up to twenty pounds. Anything in the path of the storms was knocked down and destroyed. Great floods followed and washed out roads and destroyed crops so badly needed for food. People were stranded and killed by the thousands. The repair and reconstruction of things came to a halt. The workers could only wait and brace themselves for the catastrophe of the next day.

Great critters, birds and creeping, crawling things multiplied at a phenomenal rate, and they were healthy, extra large and very aggressive.

Because of the unbelief and ungodliness of that time, the Lord reversed what He promised to Noah and his generation in: Geneses 9:2-*And the fear of you and the dread of you shall be upon every beast of the earth, and upon every fowl of the air, upon all that moveth upon the earth, and upon all the fishes of the sea.* Nature seemed to reverse itself; instead, these things such as: hateful birds, bees, scorpions, wasps, spiders, snakes, alligators and all kinds of wild life trying to avoid men, they would attack men. Black Widow and the Brown Recluse spiders would hide and then attack people seemingly out of nowhere. Many thousands died from fright and from these critters, or were tormented almost to the point of death; truly it was a time of trouble. Other unheard of things, came up out of the ruins of the destroyed cities; large lizard-like horrible creatures, and they were very fast. In fact, they could run at speeds in excess to 40 mph. When one of them would see a person, it would attack. They had a sting in their tails, and they stung men. The sting was like that of a scorpion and the pain lasted up to five months. This was all a fulfillment of what Daniel said would happen: Daniel 12:1-*'There shall be a time of trouble, such as never was since there was a nation even to that same time.* But Miles did not know that; he had laid the Bible on the shelf. In fact, it was nonsense to him.

Only a few people by comparison had guns with ammunition; most were unprotected and defenseless against all things. Even cats and dogs seemed to go mad, and they would attack and kill human beings. It was a horrifying time. Over the next two years, things got worse, almost on a daily basis. Never in all of history had there been so many things wrong; if something could go wrong, it did. To Miles, it looked as if something or someone was trying to destroy the entire human race.

China, with an Army of over two hundred million men started to make war with every one around them. Miles and The Ten had been so busy with the restoration, they had neglected rebuilding and reprogramming the great war machine.

The missile guidance systems were destroyed when the satellite, transmitting and relay system, (acronym STARS) fell to the earth. Most of the U.N.'s military aircraft was destroyed in the quake, or with the great hail storms. All the great ships and subs of the Navy were gone. When the ships and subs capsized in the shaking, raging waters of the great quake, there had been no electricity and they sank, and were forever lost with all their tremendous fire power.

When China started her move, Miles put all the air-power of the U.N in service against them; he wanted to bomb that great army out of existence, but his air-force was destroyed within three days, by hand-held surface to air missiles. Miles had not expected China to do this, therefore he was caught off guard. The great Army of China came toward Jerusalem destroying everything in its path, and there was no way Miles could stop it.

They entered the great valley out from the Mount of Olives, which had opened out for two hundred miles, during the great quake. Miles put all the forces of the world into the valley to stop them. The war machines came together: tanks, artillery, rockets, flame throwers; all weapons of destruction left to man were thrown into the engagement. It was horrible and crazy; human blood ran like a river. Fire, smoke and the stench of burned flesh moved upward, and outward; darkness and gloom hovered all over the area.

Miles and his staff went to a bunker that was hurriedly built for him on what was left of the top of Mount Olive to direct the battle. He was in touch with the commanders by radio, and ordered them to hold to the last man.

China was forcing the Army of the United Nations back toward Jerusalem. The battle raged with a terrible roar, the earth and sky were shaking. After six full twenty-four hour days, the battle was in full force, with no rest nor let-up Everything and everybody on both sides were committed. It was the most insane conflict ever witnessed! It was the battle of Armageddon spoken of in The Revelation 16:16-'*And he gathered them together into a place called in the Hebrew tongue Armageddon.*

Suddenly, there was a sound. It was like a trumpet that could be heard above all the roar. Then, the smoke and dust like a great veil, simply opened up, and rolled back, and a brown haze hung in the sky. The conflict stopped, no power was left in anyone nor anything in either of the armies; they froze in their tracks. A deathly silence prevailed, it was *so frighting!* Miles ran out of his bunker and stood looking up into the heavens. No one on earth had ever seen anything like this. All Miles could do was stand and stare at the heavens. Suddenly the sky was clear, with the exceptions of a few clouds, like a clear bright day after a storm. Then another sound from heaven, very loud, like a very loud shout. Many in the valley died from fright. it was all so awesome and distressing.

All this left no doubt in Miles' mind, this was an intervention from outer space. There was a power here, the like of which had never been witnessed by mankind. He was so frightened his knees began to knock one against the other. His mouth was dry, his tongue stuck to the roof of his mouth.

Miles had feared this, and somehow in his mind he knew something like this was going to happen. He had tried so desperately to get the nations to unite and work together and now it was too late. He knew it was over for His world and all of mankind as he had known it.

14 THE RETURN OF THE LORD

There was absolute silence; breathtaking silence which lasted for three full minutes. No leaf stirred, nothing moved ...T h e n .... in heaven there appeared a great multitude of glorified beings, similar to men, clothed in shining white robes. In front of the great throng of billions was an exceedingly glorious man, phenomenal, shining, beyond the imagination of mortal man. His glory was so that the sun was dimmed by His brightness. The great multitude came floating through the air, and there were flames of fire everywhere as they began to settle in Jerusalem and then all over the world. Mighty Angels were among them; they were different from the glorified ones, but oh so . . . beautiful! There were thousands and thousands that settled around Jerusalem; it was the greatest display of power and glory ever witnessed; it was magnificent!

The very outstanding One touched down, and His feet rested on what was left of the Mount of Olives. Then a beautiful, glorious throne appeared with the likeness of a rainbow around it, and the very outstanding One came and sat upon it. One of the mighty angels moved over and placed a brilliant, crown upon his head. An exceedingly loud voice rang out; it was like the mighty sound of a very clear-sounding trumpet, "Praise our God, He has taken His great power, and now, He shall reign on the earth as King of Kings and Lord of Lords." Then . . . it was as if the entire creation were singing; such beautiful sounds, beyond words!

Miles was so terrified; he fell to the ground, and buried his face in his hands. What on earth was happening? He wished it was a dream, but in his heart he knew this was real; this was really happening. Never had he been so scared, his heart was pounding as if it was going to jump out of his chest. His whole body was jerking and his mind was racing, everything seemed so confused and crazy. He had thought he had everything together, but this situation changed that, and he realized his world was at an end, it was over. He knew everything was completely out of his control, he was powerless against whatever it was that was happening. Fear gripped him, like he had never known in his lifetime, in fact he lost all sense of what was around him, it seemed his mind went blank, and he almost lost all awareness of reality, he felt he was going to faint. He could not breathe, his entire system was disrupted. Then, there was a voice, it sounded far off at first, then he realized it was a command, like thunder that said, "Miles! . . . come . . . stand before the throne."

Miles had no power to resist and to his amazement he was able to stand, trembling. Suddenly he felt a complete change and his entire being changed. He could see and know everything as God sees and knows, with one exception; he was powerless to change anything. He was captivated, everything was different; it was a nightmare. He knew, could see, feel and hear all things. He was totally changed by the mighty power of God, at that moment, from a mortal to an immortal being, standing naked, ashamed and very much alive before all the Glory of God, and the assembly of what was left of mankind. Suddenly the Bible became an open book to him; it was as if he had studied it all the days of his life, and was able to retain all its teachings. He was like a person with a photographic memory. He fell upon his knees before the Throne and tried to hide his face from the Lord. His body was the same in appearance, he had arms and legs; hands and feet, a mouth, nose and eyes, but he realized he was an eternal being and would exist forever. Life on earth was over for him; he was established in a different realm, and he would always be this way. God, who had made him in the beginning of his life, and had sustained him all his years, had now created him anew. He had a new life, he had a new mind, and the awful thing about it was, the open Bible would be constantly before him. He did not have to be told what this was, he knew. The verses from the Bible that prophesied this, were so clear to him. He did not have to be told who this One was; this One was not some superman creature from outer space, He was the Lord Jesus Christ, who had returned to the earth to judge and reign. The long debate over how, or when, or if He would come again, was settled once and for all. The Lord was here on the Mount of Olives; the Lord of Lords and King of Kings and there was no uncertainty whatsoever about it in the mind of Miles, nor any one else.

The Lord looked at Miles for a time, then He said, "Miles, stand and look at me."

Miles stood shaking, weeping, oh! . . . so scared, as he looked into the eyes of the Lord on the Throne. He looked at the extremely beautiful crown that was upon His head, and the rainbow of all colors around the Throne. Thousands of beautiful crowns were behind the Throne, in the hands of angels. It was all very overwhelming and frightening. The Lord's eyes were like flames of fire, yet there was a sadness in them. Miles could see the Lord did not take pleasure in what was happening. Standing beside the Throne, dressed in white robes down to their feet, were the two old Prophets and Cardinal Spilham, with many thousands that

Miles' life had affected. These were all engulfed in the Glory; time stood still. Miles had no misconception; this was his time of judgment, his time to stand before God and give account of himself. The Verses that said this:-Rom 14:11-12-*For it is written, As I live, saith the Lord, every knee shall bow to me, and every tongue shall confess to God. So then every one of us shall give account of himself to God,* flashed before him. He knew the outcome of this judgment and he could already see it. To his horror and dread he knew it would forever establish his destiny and that it would forever position him into his eternal abode. He realized, that in a moment, in the twinkle of an eye, he had been established to spend forever in everlasting existence, cast away from the Lord. The words Jesus had spoken while He was a man upon earth, in Matthew 25:46, flashed before him, *And these shall go away into everlasting punishment.* Miles knew he was one of the ones Jesus was able to see at that time, and now he could see it also.

The Lord's long, hard look was awesome. Miles realized the Lord did not hate him, but he knew he hated the sin and rejection that had ruled his life. Finally the Lord spoke, "Miles, I gave you power and glory. You had it all, but instead of giving glory to God, you have taken the things of God and lived for yourself."

Miles was trembling all over from fear, as he said, "Lord . . . Lord, have I not preached many times in your name? I gave up my desire for women, and lived a celibate life. I have done many wonderful things in the name of God. You know, I've been trying to bring the world together, so all could have plenty. Lord, you know how hard I've worked, surely, you will not condemn me for that. I've killed, yes, but I did that for a cause. I only wanted to build a proper world, so all men everywhere would have plenty. I was concerned about the sick, the downcast, the hungry, the homeless and poor. Lord, I have done many outstanding things for you, and the Virgin Mother."

"Miles . . . what you did, you did knowing full well why you were doing it."

At that moment, what Jesus had said as a man on earth flashed before Miles, and he had read it many times, but never did it register as it did in this moment. It plainly said:-John 3:18-19 *He that believes on Him* (Christ) *is not condemned: but he that believes not is condemned already. And this is the condemnation, that light is come into the world, and men loved darkness rather than light, because their deeds were evil.* Miles knew the blood of Christ that was shed upon the cross, just a short distance from where he was standing, did not cover his sins; his sins were open before God who would not, and could not tolerate sin. Why, why had he been so stupid? He could see where God had said in Exodus 12:13-*When I see the blood I will pass over you.* Now he knew what that event was in a type and a foreshadow. He knew what it had taught. Now Miles could see so plainly that the only protection for man, from the wrath of the Holy God, was the blood of the Lamb of God.

The Lord continued, "Miles, all your works were as filthy rags in my sight. I never knew you with my saving grace; my death for you was in vain, you never trusted me. You were a god to yourself, and you believed the whole world revolved around you. When you prayed in public or in private, you prayed within yourself. All that you did, you did for yourself. I was there, desiring to enter into you and live with and through you, but you never regarded me. Now, the result of what you have done will determine your degree of distress in everlasting destruction. You cannot know the extent of that as yet, but you will."

Miles knew what the Lord was saying was true. He

knew now that God was a God of truth, He could not lie. OH! to his sorrow he knew he had trampled under his ungodly feet the blood of Christ and had despised the pleading of the Holy Spirit. The words that Paul had written to the church in,-II Thessalonians 1:7-9, flashed before him, *And to you who are troubled rest with us, when the Lord Jesus shall be revealed from heaven with his mighty angels, In flaming fire taking vengeance on them that know not God, and that obey not the gospel of our Lord Jesus Christ: Who shall be punished with everlasting destruction from the presence of the Lord, and from the glory of his power.* Miles knew now what the Christians had known all along by faith, as they looked forward to this great day.

As time stood still, one by one, people began to pass before Miles as he stood before the Lord. Miles knew all these people; it was as if he was one with each of them. Many of them he had never seen while he was alive on earth, but now he knew them, and he could feel their very being as they had felt, while he had made their lives a hell on earth. He was truly reaping what he had sown. One at a time they testified, and Miles gave account to the Lord for what he had done, and the Lord judged him. He was able to see from their point of view; it was as if he was standing in their shoes, as each life he had affected passed before him. Not only did the Lord and these people condemn him, he condemned himself. It was as if he was almost limitless, and certainly all-knowing. Many of them, he had been responsible for their execution.

With Miles, there were no misunderstanding; he was loosed from the restrictions of mortal man, standing before the Lord, an open book, receiving from God the things done in his body, both good and bad; it was judgment, righteous judgment. There were no crooked lawyers, nor the influence of money, no erratic, twisted thinking, this judgment was just and true.

He realized he had really known there had to be an eternal, omnipotent, holy power that controlled, and made all that could be known and seen. Otherwise, where did it come from? Common sense had told him, the very fact it all existed, was proof enough it was made by someone all-powerful, someone eternal. The words of Paul in Romans 1:18-20-*For the wrath of God is revealed from heaven against all ungodliness and unrighteousness of men, who hold the truth in unrighteousness; Because that which may be known of God is manifest in them; for God hath shewed it unto them. For the invisible things of him from the creation of the world are clearly seen, being understood by the things that are made, even his eternal power and Godhead; so that they are without excuse*, stood out before him now. But because of the vastness of eternity, and his not being able to understand it, he had rejected God, and refused to acknowledge Him as God. He had gone his own way, and done his own thing. His world was only the things he could understand and control.

As the two old Prophets came before him, the Lord said, "I sent these men to speak to you, not only in voice, but in signs and mighty deeds, but instead of listening to them and to the pleading of the Holy Spirit speaking to you, Miles, you killed them", and He pointed to the two old glorified Prophets, who were shining like stars. "You were blinded by your own greed and lust for power. I knew your thoughts, for in me, you live, exist and have your being. I am God; I have the power to save, and the power to cast off forever. Why, do you think I came into your world and shed my blood on the cross? I did that so men everywhere could be redeemed. Miles, you trampled that blood under your ungodly feet. You were contrary to the spirit of grace that I sent forth into the world. You believed nothing. You did not realize that all that is out there in eternity, I designed for men. I created men, and have given them the power to become the Sons of God; heirs of God and joint-heirs with me. Our Father God is eternal; He has always been and He shall always be. I took upon myself the form of man, and became a man, in order to redeem the ones who would listen and be redeemed." At that moment the Word of God flashed into Miles' mind, John 1:1-5-*In the beginning was the Word, and the Word was with God, and the Word was God. The same was in the beginning with God. All things were made by him; and without him was not any thing made that was made. In him was life; and the life was the light of men. And the light shineth in darkness; and the darkness comprehended it not.* Also in verses 10-14-*'He was in the world, and the world was made by him, and the world knew him not. He came unto his own, and his own received him not. But as many as received him, to them gave he power to become the sons of God, even to them that believe on his name: Which were born, not of blood, nor of the will of the flesh, nor of the will of man, but of God. And the Word was made flesh, and dwelt among us, (and we beheld his glory, the glory as of the only begotten of the Father,) full of grace and truth.'*

Miles could now fully understand the plan and purpose of the Lord. The Lord had allotted time to men, and Miles realized he had used that time for himself. HOW COULD HE HAVE BEEN SO BLIND?

The Lord continued, "God has given me a Kingdom, an everlasting Kingdom; you could have been a part of the Kingdom, but you refused. Many, many times I stretched out my hand to you Miles, but you would not regard it. Now Miles, you can see the Lake of Fire."

Miles looked and out from the earth, about 300,000 miles, he could see another planet. It was different; it was a flaming, glowing ball of fire. He knew what it was. The verses that told of it, were before him; it was the Lake of Fire, the everlasting place for the damned.

He could see it clearly, as the Lord pointed to the burning inferno and said, "I prepared that place for Satan and his angels. You have chosen to go there and spend eternity with them, rather than with me. You . . . and you alone made your choice. I gave you my Word, and gave you the opportunity to study it, and to make a choice. I gave you a lifetime to choose and you have chosen. Now, for all the things that you have done, your portion of torment is determined forever. You are going into the Lake of Fire because you rejected my blood. Therefore! . . . depart from me, you, are cursed." Miles knew it was over, the Lord would never speak to him again.

Of the mighty angels who were hovering, circling and also standing around, one of them moved over and took Miles by the forearm, then he reached down and caught him by the upper leg. The Angel was so strong, Miles knew he could swat him into orbit with the back of his hand. Instead he lifted Miles over his head and flung him out into space.

Miles screamed, "No! . . . Lord! . . . Lord! . . . don't throw me away." As he felt himself flying out through space, he thought, "Oh! . . . if the Lord would only let me change." He screamed, "Lord, I repent . . . Lord I believe in you . . . Lord! ...Lord! forgive me, let YOUR blood that was shed on the cross wash me; Lord . . . I'm sorry for everything". He cried, he was so afraid, but his cries were too late, it was mockery, his doom was determined!

As he looked back he was able to see Mr. Mirandola standing before the Lord, and he knew he would follow shortly.

THE LAKE OF FIRE

15

Miles realized he was flying and falling out through space, toward the Lake of Fire and it was oh . . . so horrible; he was helpless! He cried and cried, he kicked and he screamed, but he was falling . . . falling . . . falling! He could see the Lake of fire, and it looked as if it was coming up to meet him. It looked like a fog of fire, similar to entering into a fog bank. As he passed into it, he realized it was very hot, and he felt pain beyond anything he had ever known, yet to his surprise he did not burn up, he did not turn to vapor and cease to exist. After the first second there, he realized sadly enough that was not the case; just as a fish is created by God to endure in water, he could now, and would forever endure in the Lake of Fire. He screamed . . . "Oh! ...God . . . Great ...God!... my torment is greater than I can bear! God, I can't stand this!--Damn you, God! I can't endure this pain, let me die, let me cease to exist." He cursed and said to himself, Damn! . . . damn! ...damn! if only I'd never been born, Damn you, God! why do you let me continue? Do you now get pleasure seeing me suffer?" It all seemed so unreasonable and even unthinkable to Miles, and he hated God for what He was subjecting him to, but his cries and cursing were futile. There was no one there to care, and certainly no one to change it; he was God's reject. He was cast out, as Jesus had said in, Matthew 25:41 -*Then shall he*

132

say also unto them on the left hand, Depart from me, ye cursed, into everlasting fire, prepared for the devil and his angels. Miles knew time would not change that fact. He was sad, to him it was grievous beyond words, very distressing. He was defeated, without God, without hope, hopelessly and helplessly lost, to be forever alone, falling, in the Lake of Fire.

He saw the Scripture flashing before him,-Deuteronomy 32:29-*O that they were wise, that they understood this, that they would consider their latter end!* It was as if God was saying, "I told you so, I warned you and you would not listen, nor would you obey."

Miles asked himself, Why was I so insane? In his mind he realized his degree of suffering would be great, because it was determined by his sin in the lifetime God had given him. He had been the worse kind of Pharisee and a hypocrite, all his sacrifice and action, was not because of the love of God nor the Church. The Scriptures flashed before him, where Jesus had warned the Pharisees and hypocrites of His day, Matthew 23:14-*Woe unto you, scribes and Pharisees, hypocrites! for ye devour widows' houses, and for a pretence make long prayer: therefore ye shall receive the greater damnation.*

In his heart, Miles knew he and everyone else in fact knew there was God by the things that are. He realized Christ had paid a great price in an attempt to save him and keep him out of this horrifying place. He also understood now, God hated his deeds, he had trampled under his ungodly feet the blood of the Son of God and had resisted the pleading of the Holy Spirit, and actually that was the unpardonable sin. Truly, he had hated God, and he had resisted even the thought that God had made all things, and controlled all things, and in fact was Lord of all things. In his lifetime, and in his actions, he certainly was not going to obey what was written in the Bible, that was irrationality to him. Now, and with every thought the Scriptures flashed before him; they were there in his mind very clear; that in itself was torture. He saw,-Romans 14:6-7 *He that regardeth the day, regardeth it unto the Lord; and he that regardeth not the day, to the Lord he doth not regard it. For none of us liveth to himself, and no man dieth to himself.* He saw also,-Ecclesiastes 3:1-8-*To every thing there is a season, and a time to every purpose under the heaven: A time to be born, and a time to die; a time to plant, and a time to pluck up that which is planted; A time to kill, and a time to heal; a time to break down, and a time to build up; A time to weep, and a time to laugh; a time to mourn, and a time to dance; A time to cast away stones, and a time to gather stones together; a time to embrace, and a time to refrain from embracing; A time to get, and a time to lose; a time to keep, and a time to cast away; A time to rend, and a time to sew; a time to keep silence, and a time to speak; A time to love, and a time to hate; a time of war, and a time of peace.'* Miles realized now clearly, God who could love with everlasting love, could also hate sin with everlasting hatred. It was payday, and he would reap forever for his sin. His sin had forever separated him from God, it was God's *time* to forever cast him away.

His features were still the same. He had a nose and as he breathed, the fire burned him way down deep inside, therefore each breath was pain, but he could not stop breathing. He had a mouth and his lips felt dry, and right away they began to swell and crack and the discomfort was awful. His tongue began to swell and stick to the roof of his mouth, it was very dry and parched. His teeth felt hot and he had an unbearable toothache. He was similar to a person out on the desert in 130 degree + temperature with no water to drink. He realized under these conditions a normal person would soon

die, but it was not so with Miles; he was no longer normal, his eternal existence was agony, distress, anguish,
misery and suffering. He had eyes and he could see,
even the planet earth and the heaven above, but his eyes
were dry and the fire burned them, the pain of his eyes
was beyond description. To make the matter worse, he
was super sensitive; every nerve of his being was react-
ing. Never could he have imagined in the furthermost
stretch of his imagination anything as horrible as this.
He had always believed it could never happen to him,
he had thought the things written about eternal damnation and suffering were written to scare people. OH!
how he did wish someone some way would have scared
him, to the point, to where he would have turned and
repented. Now, to awake in all the reality of this condition, it went beyond human understanding. But he was
no longer human, he was superhuman, and his mind
was such that he knew exactly what was transpiring.
How he did wish he could awaken and find it to be a
horrible nightmare!

He remembered his time on earth, he had been falling through space around the sun at some 67,000 mph,
and that had seemed normal; there it seemed as if he
was on solid ground, but here, there was nothing solid,
no foundation whatsoever. He was falling, tumbling,
trying his best to stabilize. It was as if he was in a spin in
an aircraft, spinning down, down, down. All his lifetime
he had not regarded the stability of his being, nor was
he thankful for the way God had created all things; he
took it all for granted and refused to give God the glory. But here and now and forever more, he would be
aware he was falling. This was now the fact of life and it
was unalterable.

The seconds dragged into minutes, and the minutes
into hours. At the end of the first day he saw the sun set,
and the darkness closed in. He wanted to go to sleep,

but he could no longer sleep; that blessing God had given to him, had now passed away. In this respect he was like God, he would never sleep again. He wept as he said to himself, If only I could go to sleep and never wake up. But after that first second when he was changed, he realized it would never be; he would be tormented and suffer every moment of every day and night forever. He cried, "God . . . Oh! God, please repent, please . . . give me another chance," he bellowed and he howled, and he yelled. But again and again the words of Jesus would flash before him, Matthew 25:41- *Then shall he say also unto them on the left hand, Depart from me, ye cursed, into everlasting fire.* Also verse-46- *And these shall go away into everlasting punishment.'*

Miles knew in his heart he was guilty in every way, and he knew why he was now in this horrible place. He realized the Word of God was true and could not be changed or broken, and he deserved what he was getting. He also understood that eventually every Christ-rejecting soul, regardless who they were, and what they were, would be coming into this place. Another Scripture came before his mind, The Revelation-21:8-*But the fearful, and unbelieving, and the abominable, and murderers, and whoremongers, and sorcerers, and idolaters, and all liars, shall have their part in the lake which burneth with fire and brimstone: which is the second death.* He could understand, death did not mean ceasing to exist and no longer to be, it meant separation, and the second death was eternal separation from God. The scriptures came,-Hebrews 9:27-*It is appointed unto men once to die, but after this the judgment.*

His mind went back and he remembered all the people he had cast into prison. He personally had supervised some of the incarcerations and he could remember the looks on their faces and the torment of being shut up, never again to be free. But all that was as nothing compared to the situation he was now in; theirs' had been temporal, his was eternal.

As the sun set on that first day, and night set in, it was dark and horrible, beyond all comprehension. Fear such as he had never known, gripped his soul and he was afraid of that dark. He knew the nights would never get any better. OH! if only he could go back and once again have the world as his audience, he would warn them day and night about this place. What a difference in his thoughts now, compared to what they had been while he was alive on the earth only a short while ago.

The night dragged on, and he watched as the moon came up over the horizon, similar to how he had watched it do so many times on earth. Looking at it only made his torment worse. There was no way he could turn things off in his mind and think on other things, and the night made it more agonizing. It seemed at night he was even more aware of his circumstances.

After a very long and fearful night, he watched the sun rise on the second day. He could remember the beginning of the new days on earth, being able to awaken, rested and feeling fresh. He was used to having the finer things ushered into him, whatever his heart desired. How pleasant it had been to have coffee and a good breakfast, but now all that was gone; he would never have a single pleasure again. He cried and he screamed, he wailed and he cursed, all the sweetness and goodness that was in him had now turned to bitterness.

Miles could see Mr. Mirandola, but there was no way he could go and speak to him. He hated him for the part he had played with him on earth. Miles could hear his cries, and his screams, and that was torture to Miles. They were both alone in their own place in the Lake of Fire. Miles realized God had made a place for everyone and everything, and now his place would forever be where he was, in the Lake of Fire, where the fire is never quenched and the worm dieth not. The Scriptures that had foretold and warned of this fact, stood out, and he realized God had given him fair warning. He could see it plainly,-Isaiah 66:24-*And they shall go forth, and look upon the carcases of the men that have transgressed against me: for their worm shall not die, neither shall their fire be quenched; and they shall be an abhorring unto all flesh.* Jesus had said,-Mark 9:43-44-*And if thy hand offend thee, cut it off: it is better for thee to enter into life maimed, than having two hands to go into hell, into the fire that never shall be quenched: Where their worm dieth not, and the fire is not quenched.*

Miles could remember how he used to drink cool, clear water, without thought, nor regard for God who gave it. His desire for water was there, but it was no longer necessary to sustain his life. He was hungry, the desire for food was there, and he could remember all the good things to eat. Now that was all gone; it also was not essential to his existence. He would continue because God committed him in his sin to this eternal death.

He thought back on remarks he had heard people make, "Well, if I go to hell, I'll have a lot of company." Nothing could be further from the truth. He   asked himself a million times, why had he not believed God? He knew now, God could not, and would not lie, yet he, in his lifetime, had called God a liar, and he, himself had lived a lie. His life was now a living hell, even worse than hell; a living devastation. He realized the ones who were now in the literal fires of hell would eventually wind up here; this was God's everlasting prison, and it was certainly no country club. The Scriptures, Psalms 9:17 and Psalms 55:15, that said, *The wicked shall be turned into hell, and all the nations that forget God,* and

Let death seize upon them, and let them go down quick into hell: for wickedness is in their dwellings, and among them, stood out before him.

During the day Miles could see the earth so clearly, and the people upon it. He did not understand it, but he could hear and see what was going on. It was torment as he watched knowing he would always be able to see. He was on the outside looking in. The words of The Revelations:-22:15-*For without are dogs, and sorcerers, and whore-mongers, and murderers, and idolaters, and whosoever loveth and maketh a lie.* It was a flashing sign before him to torture him.

16 THE JUDGEMENT SEAT OF CHRIST

Miles could see the entire throng of the redeemed, glorified Saints of Christ, who were now lifted up into Heaven. Then there was a purging fire that engulfed the entire earth. When the fire storm cleared, the people on earth who were still alive in their mortal flesh, along with all the fleshly beings came crawling out of the caves and holes of the earth. The ones who survived, endured because they took shelter in places that were untouched by the purging fire. Everything and everybody that could not endure the fire was destroyed, only a few thousand were left. Mankind in the flesh was back to a new beginning, and the earth was enlarged and cleansed.

In a short time, the earth was as the Garden of Eden; it was beautiful, uncontaminated and pure. God's power to re-create was marvelous to behold, although to watch the change only brought more misery to Miles.

He watched as the atmospheric conditions changed and the weather became perfect; not too hot, not too cold. The sky was bright: no smog, nor smoke, not a cloud. Everything was lovely, and so desirable, a heaven on earth. The ones who were still alive in their mortal flesh, Miles knew could live on for a long time. He knew them each and everyone and was able to know what they felt. He was as God in that sense, only he was limited, God had changed Miles' brain; he knew every one of these by name. It was awful to be there in his mind with them, yet in his very being he, himself was in the Lake of Fire. Although his mind could interact with others, the torment of the Lake of Fire would never let up for one moment.

Again, Miles saw the Throne in Heaven, and the Lord sitting upon that Throne. First, he saw Satan and his angels as they were gathered together and compelled to stand powerless before the Throne. There was not a word spoken, the Lord sat and looked at them, then with a nod as Miles watched, a great pit was opened. It was like a burning, churning, boiling flow of lava, and it seemed as if it went into the center of the earth. The mighty angels laid hands on Satan and his, lifted them up, and brutally, without mercy, cast them screaming, kicking and cursing into that pit, and the pit was sealed and disappeared.

Then Miles could see the redeemed still up in the heavens. There was a great throng of billions, and many of them were in shining white robes. Others were naked with no covering whatsoever. Miles could see and he knew that all of these were there because they had accepted the blood of Christ, and their sins were forgiven and covered. He watched and saw the clothed and the unclothed as they came one at a time, and stood alone before the Throne. Again time stood still for them, but not for Miles, his days and nights dragged as the judgment transpired; he was forced to witness and to interact. Miles knew this was the Judgment Seat of Christ, the judgment of the redeemed. It was not a judgment of sin, but rather of works. The Scripture that foretold of this event came into his mind,-II Corinthians 5:10-*For we* (the saved) *must all appear before the judgment seat of Christ; that everyone may receive the things done in his body, according to that he hath done, whether it be good or bad.*

Many of these people standing there had lived during

Miles' lifetime, and many of them he had read about. Miles saw the two old Prophets come, one at a time, bow their heads, then fall upon their knees before the Lord. The Lord blessed them, and commended them, saying, "Well done my good, faithful and true servants, you have been faithful unto death with the things I committed unto you, now, I crown you rulers over many things." One of the mighty angels came forward and placed a crown upon their heads and crowned them Kings. Miles knew they were now Kings in the Kingdom of God, which kingdom is an everlasting kingdom. All of the angels and the redeemed sang praises to them and they were given by the Lord new names. Miles knew just as he would be forever in the lake of fire, even so these two would be in all the Glory of God, and the awful thing, Miles not only could see them, he could feel the joy they felt, but that had an adverse effect upon him. It was so sad to Miles, he thought within himself, what would I give if I could change places with them! But OH! Oh! The horror as he realized, now it will always be as it is, it is over and done. His mind went back when he stood on the steps of the temple and yelled, "Shoot them." If only, some way he could change that, but he knew he couldn't, he would remember and that also would always forever and forever torture him. Miles thought back, I was there, I could have changed, but the reality was he didn't. There that day, he realized he had made an eternal choice. It troubled his mind now, but he knew there was nothing he could do, to change it.

He saw David, and as David came, behind him came Uriah the Hittite and Bath-Sheba his wife. The three of them came one after the other and approached the Throne and bowed their heads before the Lord. Miles could feel, and did relive the time with David as he turned his back upon the Lord and went after his own lust in the matter with Bath-Sheba. He could feel the internal sorrow of David's soul as he grieved over putting forth his hand and taking what belonged to another. Then it was as if Miles was within Beth-Sheba as she was brought before the King. Also he could feel the grief of Uriah and did in his mind relive the time with him.

Then he saw David come and fall upon his face before the Throne and cry unto the Lord over his sin against Uriah the Hittite. Uriah the Hittite approached and fell with him and threw his arms around David saying, "I forgive you, David, my brother." There on their knees they embraced and wept before the Lord. Bath-Sheba moved over to them and fell with her arms around them, weeping. The Lord spoke, ever so kindly, "My grace is sufficient for all of you. Be at peace, behold I shall make all things new, and you will remember no more forever, but you have your rewards." Again Miles watched as the angels moved over and placed the crowns of Life upon their heads. The matter was closed, buried beneath the cross of Christ, to be remembered no more, and each of them were assigned to their everlasting portion.

Miles saw John the Baptist, the Apostles, Moses, Elijah, Abraham, Cardinal Spilham, the Pope, Father Kolas who had raised him. He watched as they came and stood before the Throne. He saw as their eyes looked into the Lord's eyes. There was rejoicing as the Lord would say, "Well done, good and faithful servant, you have been faithful over a few things, now I make you forever ruler over many things." Many were crowned with crowns. The words of Paul, that were pinned on his dungeon wall before his death, flashed into Miles' mind, II Timothy 4:7-8-*I have fought a good fight, I have finished my course, I have kept the faith. Henceforth there is laid up for me a crown of righteousness, which the*

Lord, the righteous judge, shall give me at that day: and not to me only, but unto all them also that love his appearing.

Also, there was weeping, wailing and gnashing of teeth on the part of many, because of the hypocritical lives they had lived. Some of them had been pastors and teachers and had committed adultery, or ruled over the work of the Lord by force.

Miles saw one pastor, in his lifetime he had pastored a large church for 35 years before the Lord returned. He had ruled the church with a rod of iron and any one in the congregation who dared to oppose him would be denounced and litterly dismissed from the church. Many, many good people were hindered by his ministry, he was not a servant, he was a dictator. Miles watched him as he approched the throne, so proud and airrogant. The Lord looked at him and the Lord' eyes were hard as he said, "Frank, I gave you a place in one of my wonderful strong churches, but instead of following me and putting me forth as Lord of the church, you took control by force. You hendered these lives," and he turned and pointed to the many that were wronged and had stumbled because of his example. "Frank, this is what you could have inherited" and there flashed before him a wonderful exaulted position in the Kingdom of God. Miles could see it as Frank saw it. All the sudden his conceited and inflated attude changed. As the truth dawned in his mind he realized he had waisted his life and thrown away his opportunity to serve God. The Lord said, "Frank you were not serving me, you were serving yourself. Now, take your place with the hypocrites."

Frank wept and he wailed as he departed from the Throne and took his place.

There were others who had stolen, lied and cheated. All the reprobate things they had done, the Lord knew about, and they knew that He knew. Miles was able to know and he could feel what they felt as the truth was judged by the Lord. They could not say they were without instructions in life. But they had rebelled and turned every one to his own way. Paul's teaching to the church flashed across Miles' mind, Galatians 5:16-26-*This I say then, Walk in the Spirit, and ye shall not fulfil the lust of the flesh. For the flesh lusteth against the Spirit, and the Spirit against the flesh: and these are contrary the one to the other: so that ye cannot do the things that ye would. But if ye be led of the Spirit, ye are not under the law. Now the works of the flesh are manifest, which are these; Adultery, fornication, uncleanness, lasciviousness, idolatry, witchcraft, hatred, variance, emulations, wrath, strife, seditions, heresies, envyings, murders, drunkenness, revellings, and such like: of the which I tell you before, as I have also told you in time past, that they which do such things shall not inherit the kingdom of God.* Miles could understand that these acts were sins that were covered by the Blood, but that time was lost because of the wrong doing, and the things that could have been were lost also. They did not inherit the Kingdom of God in the way they could have; they were there, but they were the least of the least because of their deeds. Miles could see and understand so clearly Jesus' words,-Matthew 5:19-*Whosoever therefore shall break one of these least commandments, and shall teach men so, he shall be called the least in the kingdom of heaven.* In addition to that he could see,-I Corinthians 3:13-15-*Every man's work shall be made manifest: for the day shall declare it, because it shall be revealed by fire; and the fire shall try every man's work of what sort it is. If any man's work abide which he hath built thereupon, he shall receive a reward. If any man's work shall be burned, he shall suffer loss: but he himself shall be saved; yet so as by fire.* Oh! how Miles did wish he had taken time to see

and understand this teaching while he was alive. He realized he had walked after his flesh all his life. He was
never born of the Spirit. But these were born of the
Spirit, yet they had walked after the flesh and grieved
the Holy Spirit of God that was within them. What
Jesus said in John 3:6-7-was there before Miles, *That
which is born of the flesh is flesh; and that which is born of
the Spirit is spirit. Marvel not that I said unto thee, Ye
must be born again.* Miles understood these were born
again people, who had lived like the Devil in the flesh.
He could hear the Lord say to them, "Have your portion with the hypocrites, you accepted my sacrifice for
your sin, then you turned and walked in the flesh and
after the things of the flesh; you are saved as by fire, all
your works are burned." Inside the deep confines of the
soul, each and everyone knew this judgment was just
and according to Truth. Miles was able to experience
their feelings, and understand their emotions as if he
was inside them. It was awful for him. It was all very
clear to him; God had given to all, a lifetime with a free
will. In that one life . . . each and everyone had determined for themselves, by their own volition, their eternal position forever. Standing there, some naked and
ashamed, the bottom line was, they had no one to
blame but themselves and the Devil. Therefore on the
one hand, for some it was glorious, on the other hand,
for some it was sad. They wept and they wailed as the
Truth dawned, but it was over; what was done was
done forever.

There were four seats, two on either side of the
Throne and one by one those four seats were filled with
Kings.

Again the words of Jesus flashed before Miles,-Reve-
lation 4:21-*To him that overcometh will I grant to sit
with me in my throne, even as I also overcame, and am set
down with my Father in his throne.*

Beyond those four, were twenty-four seats and one by one those seats were filled. Out further from the Throne was a great multitude, beyond number. It looked like a great sea of glass, so calm and peaceful. These were divided into twenty-four nations and over each nation were Kings, Lords and Priests, rulers of thousands, of hundreds, of fifties and so forth. Of the nations, some were restricted to planet earth, others were loosed to go out into eternity and do whatever their heart could desire. Eternity, space and endless time were theirs. They were eternal, set in eternity, loosed into the glorious liberty of the sons of God.

Miles disappointment within himself was crushing. He wept and he wept. He realized the exalted position he had held in life had only been a curse to him. Why had he not been born without eyes to see, maybe he could have seen. Or why had he not been paralyzed and dependent upon others, maybe he could have discovered the Truth of life, and not be in this eternal state of the cursed. He realized many who were handicapped in their lifetime were actually blessed, because in their suffering they had drawn near to God, and now they had their reward.

After the judgment was over, the nations were then established upon the earth as a result of that judgment. The entire throng returned to the earth and the Spirit of God was in fact poured upon all flesh. Miles could see there was joy and peace as each accepted their lot. No one was out of place; each had their own and they were happy. But it was not so with Miles, he would always remember and be tormented by the things that could have been.

The earth was established for the Thousand Year Reign of Christ. Miles could see and understand the prophecy of Joel,-Joel 2:21-29 *Fear not, O land; be glad and rejoice: for the LORD will do great things. Be not afraid, ye beasts of the field: for the pastures of the wilderness do spring, for the tree beareth her fruit, the fig tree and the vine do yield their strength. Be glad then, ye children of Zion, and rejoice in the LORD your God: for he hath given you the former rain moderately, and he will cause to come down for you the rain, the former rain, and the latter rain in the first month. And the floors shall be full of wheat, and the fats shall overflow with wine and oil. And I will restore to you the years that the locust hath eaten, the cankerworm, and the caterpiller, and the palmerworm, my great army which I sent among you. And ye shall eat in plenty, and be satisfied, and praise the name of the LORD your God, that hath dealt wondrously with you: and my people shall never be ashamed. And ye shall know that I am in the midst of Israel, and that I am the LORD your God, and none else: and my people shall never be ashamed. And it shall come to pass afterward, that I will pour out my spirit upon all flesh; and your sons and your daughters shall prophesy, your old men shall dream dreams, your young men shall see visions: And also upon the servants and upon the handmaids in those days will I pour out my spirit.* Also Miles could comprehend the fulfillment of, Isaiah 2:2-4-*And it shall come to pass in the last days, that the mountain of the LORD's house shall be established in the top of the mountains, and shall be exalted above the hills; and all nations shall flow unto it. And many people shall go and say, Come ye, and let us go up to the mountain of the LORD, to the house of the God of Jacob; and he will teach us of his ways, and we will walk in his paths: for out of Zion shall go forth the law, and the word of the LORD from Jerusalem. And he shall judge among the nations, and shall rebuke many people: and they shall beat their swords into plowshares, and their spears into pruninghooks: nation shall not lift up sword against nation, neither shall they learn war any more.*

17 THE THOUSAND YEAR REIGN

Miles could see as Jerusalem was established once again on the earth with all the glory of God in her midst. The Lord's Throne was placed there, and David was next to Him on His right hand.

Miles was fully aware of the fact that this was the Kingdom of Heaven spoken of in the Bible. He knew it would reign on the earth for one thousand years, until every jot and tittle of the Word of God was fulfilled.

He saw as each nation took it's place on the earth and there was peace and joy, such joy! Everything and everyone on earth praised the Lord. The knowledge of the Glory of the Lord covered the earth as the water covered the seas. The great deserts of the past were no more, they bloomed and yielded their fruits bountifully. A mist went up at night and watered the new vegetation the Lord created, it was all so perfect. No weed would grow; it was a restoration of the Garden of Eden that extended all over the earth. All the farmers had to do was cultivate the ground, plant, prune and gather the fruits. The growing season was 365 days per year. There was an abundance for all. If the farmers desired they could plant new fields, and grow new fruits and vegetables, whatsoever; the possibility was limitless.

Nation did not lift up sword against nation, neither did they study war any more. The Spirit of God was upon all flesh; no creeping crawling critter, nor snake would bite, no dog would bark. The lamb and the lion would lay together. The lion would eat straw like an ox. A little child would play with and, love a rattlesnake; nothing would hurt nor destroy. There was no killing, no thief to break through and steal. Perfect safety prevailed and no one nor anything was afraid. Each and everyone stayed in their rightful place; never in the history of mankind had there been such satisfaction and understanding with perfect order.

Miles could see churches, with pastors and teachers. These met once a week, upon the first day of the week, the Lord's day There were those left in the flesh who had never accepted Christ as Saviour. Babies were born to them, and with no sickness nor death, millions of new souls came into being in a short time. Even though there was no more sin, these new souls needed to accept Christ, be born again and given a Spiritual nature.

Miles could feel that in the hearts of the pastors and teachers there was a real burden to bring these unsaved souls under the sound of the Gospel, to give them a chance to accept the Lord and become spiritual. Although the Spirit of God was upon them, He was not within them, and it was a must that they accept the blood of Christ and be born again.

Miles could see and he knew that even though the knowledge of the Glory of the Lord covered the earth, the inherent nature of Adam and his fall was still alive and well. Miles realized that these glorified saints knew the time would come when Satan would be released, that these souls would have their hour of temptation, therefore it was a burden to see all born again.

He could see great revival meetings, and men such as the glorified Apostle Paul would preach. There were no compromising, side-stepping, hireling preachers there; they were all in their lot with the hypocrites. Such preaching and singing! Many thousands accepted Christ and were baptized in the crystal clear waters of the beautiful flowing rivers. It was all very wonderful to the ones on earth, but such sorrow to Miles.

Miles watched as once a year, the ones representing each nation would go into Jerusalem for the Feast of Tabernacles. The Kings, Lords and Priests would bring their gifts to the King of Kings and Lord of Lords. There would be a time of feasting and rejoicing known only to the ones present. Only the ones who had earned the right were permitted there. Miles could understand what Jesus meant when he prophesied of this time, in, Matthew 8:11-*And I say unto you, That many shall come from the east and west, and shall sit down with Abraham, and Isaac, and Jacob, in the kingdom of heaven.'*

Miles watched, and oh . . . how his heart did yearn to be a part of that Kingdom! Such torment, to be able to see, to hear, to feel, and to know, yet for him it would never be. He was without hope forever; what loss! sad . . . sad . . . sad . . . but yet so true and very real. He knew this same fate awaited every Christ-rejecting soul ever born. OH!... if there was only some way to go back to them and warn them. He would do anything, he would cry in the streets, and beg them to be saved, if he only had the chance. But he knew it would never be. He had his chance, he had his time.

The Scriptures flashed into Miles' mind,-Isaiah 53:10-*When thou shalt make his soul an offering for sin, he shall see his seed, he shall prolong his days, and the pleasure of the LORD shall prosper in his hand.* Miles knew that when Jesus hung on the cross, dying for sin, He was able to see what Miles was seeing now. He cried to himself, "OH! WHY?—OH! WHY?—did I not see it before it was everlastingly too late. It was there in the Book of God all of my days. If only I had used common sense and believed it, if only ego, greed and selfishness had not been my reason for existing!"

Miles watched and time for him dragged into years. One hundred years went by, two hundred; they passed . . . oh . . . so slowly and full of suffering.

At the end of a very long one thousand years, one day Miles saw the Pit that was in the heart of the earth opened. He watched as Satan and all his angels were loosed. Miles watched them go out and once again in spirit, cover the earth. Once again that spirit of the Devil became the great lying voice, and a tempter. As a raging lion he went about seeking the unsaved and trying to hinder the glorified ones, and the saved. In a very short time there was a great multitude of the unsaved who rose up in rebellion against Christ. They worked to disrupt, on every hand, and at every turn; things began to happen and turn ungodly. There was rebellion once again against God and the servants of God. Many of the people still in the flesh, took a hard stand against the servants of God. They began to kill animals and to eat flesh. Certain beasts turned violent and began to destroy the unity and tranquility that had prevailed for so long. Murder, rape and theft once again began to occur. Miles watched as the influence of the spirit of disobedience gathered together a mighty army, and they came and assembled themselves around Jerusalem, but it was all short lived. There was a mighty voice that rang out from Heaven, as the great wrath of Almighty God was kindled. It was so powerful and so loud that the entire earth and the heavens shook. It said in no uncertain terms, "It is enough, it is over and done." In a moment, Christ and all the glorified, redeemed were caught up into the heavens. At that same instant also, all who had been born again during the Thousand Year Reign were caught up with them into Heaven, and changed from mortal to immortal.

18 THE GREAT WHITE THRONE

Miles watched as a Great White Throne appeared in Heaven; the glory of it was so bright it lit the entire universe and the sun seemed dim by comparison. It appeared as if it was established upon a large raised platform with circular steps leading up to it. Behind and on the sides, shaped as a horse shoe was a great elevation, like a choir loft. The redeemed were fanned back and situated on that spot overlooking the Throne from behind and the sides. Mighty angels were there all around. It was all so awesome, and the glory was such, that no mortal could stand alive before it. A fire went out from the Throne and consumed everything, and everyone on earth disappeared. The earth became a molten ball of fire, the oceans boiled, and everything exploded, even the sun. The earth and the sun, as they were, passed away.

It was amazing for Miles to watch as everything cleared, then he could see all the electrons, protons and neutrons that made up the atoms, as they were reassembled, and reacted to the will and the direction of God. When the new earth was finished, it was beautiful, and there was no more sun nor sea.

The Great White Throne and He that sat upon it was the Light, and that Light went out forever. Miles saw all the bodies that had been in graves, on earth and in the sea; they came forth as the atoms were assembled into new bodies. He could see all the souls that had been in hell from the beginning of time, as they each and everyone took on their resurrected body, and lived again in the same fashion as he and Mr. Mirandola. Satan also, and his angels were changed; they were all grouped together. All who were not covered by the blood of Christ were gathered before that Throne. It was easy for Miles to understand this was the judgment bar of God, the judgment of the unsaved. There were books there, and then yet another book, which Miles could see was the Book of Life. The scriptures that prophesied of this time flashed before Miles in The Revelation- 20:11-15, *And I saw a great white throne, and him that sat on it, from whose face the earth and the heaven fled away; and there was found no place for them. And I saw the dead, small and great, stand before God; and the books were opened: and another book was opened, which is the book of life: and the dead were judged out of those things which were written in the books, according to their works. And the sea gave up the dead which were in it; and death and hell delivered up the dead which were in them: and they were judged every man according to their works. And death and hell were cast into the lake of fire. This is the second death. And whosoever was not found written in the book of life was cast into the lake of fire.*

First Miles saw the old Devil, Satan who now had a body similar to a man. Miles watched him as he climbed the steps, trembling and afraid, and bowed before the Throne. He heard the Lord say, "Satan, I created time, then I created you and yours, and gave all of you a great kingdom of worlds, planets, places unlimited, in the great eternal macrocosm that I had created and maintained. You were free to come and go, you had it all. I had pleasure in you and yours, you were so beautiful. But you were not satisfied, you wanted to raise yourself above the Throne of God. Satan, that was sin! I cannot and will not tolerate sin. I destroyed your worlds and turned them upside down and they became a vast desolation. I disembodied you and all who chose to follow you, and there was darkness and I elected to let it be for a long, long time."

"I reestablished the earth, and made it a testing ground, so each and everyone you had taken down could be tested and tried in time. I knew all, and I knew what they would do, I alone am God and in me all things exist. It was my desire though, that each and every soul in the Kingdom of the Son should be free to choose what they would do and what they would be. I released you in spirit with your angels for the purpose of righteous judgment. I created two bodies and placed two of the disembodied spirits into what is now known as Adam and Eve. I did that in order to replenish the earth only. I gave you limited power over the world that evolved upon planet earth. You lied, you cheated, and deceived, you took a stand contrary to my nature and desire. All were influenced by you from the cradle to the grave, thereby creating a situation, forcing each and every soul to choose between good and evil. It was not in the power of man to overcome the temptations you set before them, therefore I elected to provide a sacrifice of my blood to cover their sins.

One by one those disembodied spirits were placed into a body, and given another chance, a lifetime to choose. The billions who were born, were not of their Mother and Father; they only passed through them, back upon the stage of time, free moral agents with a choice. I allowed you to have power in spirit to enter into as many as would allow you. It was not my will, but I desired a Kingdom of souls who would choose me; therefore I permitted it to happen. As I said in my Word in-Proverbs 8:17-*I love them that love me; and those that seek me early shall find me.* I made it possible for them to find me through the death of Christ on the cross."

"I gave the offspring of Adam and Eve a Book, the Bible. In that Book, for almost four thousand years, I foretold what would be done, first in shadows and in types, then in signs and symbols, rituals and ceremonies. In other places I declared plainly what would happen and what had happened in such a way that any searching mind could find me. I told plainly of the virgin birth, even named the city where Christ Jesus would be born, more than 710 years before he was born. Not only did I tell where, I told how, through the miraculous conception of a virgin. I also showed before hand where, how and when the Lord would die. The Book known as the Scriptures were fulfilled with the life and example of Jesus in time. But in the face of this overwhelming evidence, all men sinned and came short of the glory of God. I chose the entire nation of Israel and spoke to them face to face, but regardless of my teachings, they turned every man to his own way. They were instructed to offer offerings, to picturized and foreshadow the death of Christ. And in so doing they were to roll their sins forward each and every year, until the Christ came and paid the price once and for all. By faith the ones who accepted the blood of Christ looked forward to His coming. The ones who did not were condemned and you see them standing here this day."

"In my time, I entered into a body as a baby, born of a virgin, with God as my Father and the blood of God in my veins. I grew up in that world among men, as I had foretold in the Book. I came and spoke to mankind, showing many infallible signs and supernatural things that testified in the most powerful way. Then I died on a cross, shed my blood, the blood of the only begotten son God, to cover all sin forever; giving them all the opportunity to choose between you and me; which is eternal life, or eternal death."

"If they chose me, I forever redeemed them through the shed blood, and gave them my Spirit within, so they could choose and do what they would. I promised a reward if they would take up their cross, deny themselves and follow me. You see them, the billions of them here with me this day. Others chose you, and yours, even knowing it was just for a short time. You can now see the Lake of Fire. Satan, I created that place for you and your angels. You and yours will spend eternity there. You, because you did not choose to obey me, the rest, because they too followed you and rejected my blood that was shed to pay for their sin. Sin will never be a part of my Kingdom; it has now, and will forever have it's place in the Lake of Fire."

Satan fell on his face screaming before the Throne. He cried, "God, please don't turn me away. Please don't throw me away forever. You have the power to forgive. OH! . . . please God forgive. You are a God of mercy, please . . . forgive."

"Satan, I gave you my Word. You knew it and you have taken as many as you could into perdition. It is impossible for the Word of God to be broken; therefore I will do what I said I would do... Depart! . . . from me you cursed."

Satan screamed, kicked and cursed as one of the mighty angels moved over, picked him up, and threw him out into space toward the Lake of Fire. Then the Scripture flashed before Miles in The Revelation 20:10- *And the devil that deceived them was cast into the lake of fire and brimstone, where the beast* (Miles) *and the false prophet* (Mr. Mirandola) *are, and shall be tormented day and night for ever and ever.*

Miles saw him coming, he saw him enter into the fire.

There was no way he could go to him, nor communicate with him. He could hear his screams, his groaning and cursing. Miles knew God's justice was done. Satan had asked for it, and he got it, all in due time. A portion of Scripture flashed before Miles in, Ecclesiastes 8:11- *Because sentence against an evil work is not executed speedily, therefore the heart of the sons of men is fully set in them to do evil.* Miles realized how foolish he had been to make a ridicule of sin.

He saw the rich man that Jesus spoken about in the Gospel of Luke. Miles knew him, and could feel his very being. Miles knew he had been in Hell for thousands of years, and now he was brought out to stand before the Judgment Bar of God. This judgment would determine his place, punishment and suffering for his sin, in the Lake of Fire.

Miles recognized Cardinal Frank Reeves, who he had appointed over the Church in Jerusalem, to replace Cardinal Spilham. He was no longer proud and arrogant, rather he fell upon his face and shook all over as he cried. He raised upon his knees and said, pleading with the Lord, "Lord, I served you faithfully in my life, you know that.

"Frank you were not serving me, you were serving yourself. The riches and power of the Church blinded you. You loved the praise, the power and prestige, the pomp and glory. I was there in Spirit but you shut me out and walked in your own way. Many, many times I streched out my hand to you, but you refused my council. Now, Cardinal Frank Reeves, you have made your chose, you will spend eternity in the Lake of Fire. Not because I hate you, but because I hate your sin, and you refused to let me cover it with my blood.'

The Cardinal fell kicking and screaming upon his face. One of the mighty angels came over picked him up and flung him out through space as he had Miles, Mr.Mirandola and Satan.

Billions and billions who had chosen *to live for themselves* stood powerless before the Lord, as Miles had done. For them time stood still. They were weeping, wailing, groaning, cursing and screaming. The great cry from so many roared and the sound was horrifying. The sound went on and on and Miles knew that sound would go on forever, and that he would be forced to listen to it. Great sorrow and disappointment prevailed as the twisted lives of these reprobates appeared. It was so sad to Miles and he could feel what each and everyone felt. It was as if he was one within each of them. He could now understand how grieved God had been as He looked upon the wickedness of man. He even wondered how God had tolerated it as long as He had. Miles knew that one by one these would be coming into the Lake of Fire, with him and Mr. Mirandola. These lost souls, would be forever alone, forever tormented, forever falling. They would take up their eternal abode, surrounded by all the suffering and moaning and groaning, the cursing and screaming, the awful sound that would always be among God's rejects, who were doomed and damned forever. All had one thing in common, they had rejected and scoffed at the grace of God and the Christ that God gave to save them, therefore the wrath of God with out mercy would always abide upon them, because of sin. The words of Jesus stood out so plainly in the mind of Miles in-John 3:18-19, *He that believeth on him* (Jesus the Christ) *is not condemned: but he that believeth not is condemned already, because he hath not believed in the name of the only begotten Son of God. And this is the condemnation, that light is come into the world, and men loved darkness rather than light, because their deeds were evil.'*

One by one, every so slowly, Miles saw them climb the steps, come and stand, then bow before the Great White Throne. The Scriptures flashed into Miles' mind,-Romans 14:11-*'For it is written, As I live, saith the Lord, every knee shall bow to me, and every tongue shall confess to God.'*

As the billions came one by one Miles saw them and knew each one by name. He watched as a young man whose name was Mark Clark came before the Throne. Mark had been in hell for well over a thousand years, all through the Judgment Seat of Christ and the Thousand Year Reign of Christ. Now Miles could see him and he knew him as he was brought out to stand before the Great White Throne of judgment. In Mark's short life time of eighteen years on earth he was a spoiled brat. Because he was such an unruly young man the Pastor had suggested to his father that he discipline Mark before it was everlastingly too late. Mr. Clark was very successful, in so much that he had great influence over the people of the town, and he certainly was not going to be told how to raise his son. He had supplied most of the money to build the local church, and that gave him the misguided idea that he should control what was said and done in that church.

One morning the Pastor took a text from the Scriptures in,-Proverbs 22:6-*Train up a child in the way he should go: and when he is old, he will not depart from it.* He continued his sermon and took another Scripture instructing the congregation on the discipline of children. He used, Proverbs-23:13-14, *Withhold not correction from the child: for if thou beatest him with the rod, he shall not die. Thou shalt beat him with the rod, and shalt deliver his soul from hell.*

Mark's father took offense to the preaching of the Pastor that morning and pulled his wife and son out of the church, and stopped attending altogether. Mark grew up not knowing what the word no meant. When he graduated from school at eighteen, his father bought him a nice new convertible car. It was another toy for him, and because of the car he was popular with many of the kids his age. He became wild and was extremely selfish; he was always in and out of trouble with the local law.

Miles could see Mark, in fact it was as if he was there with him, yet Miles was still conscious of the fact he was in the Lake of Fire. But his mind was within Mark on one beautiful, clear, sunny afternoon. Mark picked up two other boys for a joy ride down the highway from their home town. On the way out of town, they stopped and picked up a case of beer. The store keeper would not say no to them, because of Mark's father's influence.

They took the beer and started drinking as they drove down the highway. Mark was drunk when he decided it would be fun to drive the new car from the back seat with a rope. So they all got into the back seat, with the rope tied to the steering wheel. Mark sat in the middle and pulled the throttle full on and away they went, yelling and laughing and acting very crazy. The car had reached eighty five m.p.h. when he lost control. It left the highway and Mark never knew what happened, until he woke up in the fires of hell. From hell he could see the earth, just as Miles could now see from the Lake of Fire.

Mark watched as they prepared his body for the funeral and for the grave. He saw his father and mother weep and wail at the funeral. He heard the newly elected Pastor say, "Now beloved, we know that even now Mark is walking the streets of gold in heaven." The Pastor said that trying to entice Mark's father and mother to come back into the church; he was not concerned with the truth nor the souls of men.

Miles could feel the horror of what Mark felt in the flames of hell. He could see and hear him as he would wail and cry. He screamed at the Pastor, as if he could hear him, "Tell them the truth, you compromising bas-

tard, damn you, don't say what they want to hear!"
Miles could feel and understand that Mark realized the
hireling preacher was destroying souls, and that many
of them under the sound of his voice would wind up in
Hell.

Mark had spent all those long years in hell, tormented in the flames day and night. Time did not stand still
for the ones in Hell. They were disembodied spirits,
and the torment of Hell was a spiritual thing, whereas
Miles was established in his everlasting body.

Durning that time Miles could see that Hell had to
be enlarged, as the Scriptures had said, in Isaiah 5:14-
15-*Therefore hell hath enlarged herself, and opened her
mouth without measure: and their glory, and their multitude, and their pomp, and he that rejoiceth, shall descend into it. And the mean man shall be brought down,
and the mighty man shall be humbled, and the eyes of the
lofty shall be humbled.*

There were so many souls that went into Hell at the
last days before the Rapture, it was because there was a
great moral break down within the homes of the nations, and a lukewarm, compromising attitude within
the churches.

When the Great White Throne appeared, Miles could
see Mark, and it was as if he was within him. Mark felt
himself being changed, and as he re-entered his resurrected body, he was caught up to stand and give account to God for what he had done.

As Mark climbed the steps to the Throne he saw his
father and mother, they were among that great throng
of the redeemed. When his father saw him he went running to him, crying,"My son! my son! what have I done
to you?"

Mark cursed him, he hated him, he believed because
of his father and the way he had lived before him, he
had gone to hell. Mark's father wailed and wailed there
before the assembled universe.

Miles was forced to relive through all this with Mark and his father; it was horrible for Miles. There was no relief as one after the other of these cases would come to his mind. In no way could Miles escape this torture, it was madness and always negative, this was just another segment of his degree of punishment, and it would always be, day and night forever. Sad, sad for Miles, but he and he alone had made his choice.

Miles could see all those who had chosen not to regard God: all the un-righteous, wicked, covetous, the malicious and the fornicators. He saw also ones full of envy, murder, debate, deceit, malignity, backbiters, haters of God, the despiteful, proud, boasters, inventors of evil things, disobedient to parents, without understanding, without natural affection, implacable and unmerciful liars. These came one by one, and stood before the Just, Holy and Almighty God. With many of them Miles had been contemporary, others he had read about in History. He saw the old bloody Dogs of Rome, who had persecuted the Christians, also the ones of Adolph Hitler's days who had so troubled the world, and killed so many. One at a time they came, and stood alone before the Throne.

He saw another young man who had committed suicide after wrecking his father's car, rather than face the father. He had the misguided concept that death would end it all, not knowing that death was only the beginning of life in heaven or in hell. Occasionally there would be one of the redeemed, a relative or friend, who would come, fall before the Throne and beg for a soul. There was weeping and wailing on the part of the redeemed over their failures. Fingers were pointed and words,"You! . . . you failed me . . . you knew, why did you not reach out to me, why did you not correct me?' The failures and loose living on the part of the saved were heard. It was oh . . . so awful as time for them stood still. Miles could understand what Jesus meant when He said in Matthew-12:36-37-*But I say unto you, That every idle word that men shall speak, they shall give account thereof in the day of judgment. For by thy words thou shalt be justified, and by thy words thou shalt be condemned.*

The redeemed were mourning, grieving, pleading, begging; some even offered to trade places, to give themselves for loved ones. There were fathers pleading for wives, for sons and daughters, wives for their husbands, sons and daughters, grandparents for children and grandchildren, but it was too late. The ones who had rejected Christ, were taken without mercy, and thrown alive into the Lake of Fire. Miles could see them coming, tumbling, falling, screaming, kicking. Many were cursing their parents, their pastors, teachers and God.

When it was over and done, The Lord said, "Behold I make all things new", and the former things were wiped away, to be remembered no more.

At that time Miles was able to look back before Adam and Eve, when Satan and all of them together had stood before God. He could see there was a Lamb of God offered for sin. They all had seen and known at that time, then God had wiped all the former things from their minds, and one by one they entered once again on the scene of time; with the blood of Adam. They were given another body and another chance, but many of them failed to regard God and His love as their true nature was manifest. Now they were in their rightful places forever.

For those who chose to accept the Blood of Christ, there would be no more remembrance of the former things. There would be no more sorrow, pain nor death; they were redeemed, the blood of Christ covered their sin. But the ones who had rejected Christ would remember, be hungry, be thirsty, would fall, would be

alone, tormented day and night forever and ever.
Amen . . . Miles knew, he was one of those.

THE HOLY CITY

19

Miles watched as the Great White Throne disappeared, then he saw an object coming down from God out of heaven. At first, it looked like a great mountain, and on its top there was something four square, sparkling like a very expensive diamond. As it approached, the Light grew brighter and brighter. It was extremely brilliant and that manifestation of Light went out in every direction forever, even to the Lake of Fire where Miles existed.

The object came to a place between the Lake of Fire and the new Earth, about 3,000,000 miles from each, then stopped. Miles could then see that it was in fact, a foursquare City set on the top of a beautiful, high mountain. He watched as the entire order of the macrocosm changed; galaxies and super galaxies took on a definite new orbit, everything out in the eons of infinity began to circle very orderly around the City.

Miles studied the City, it reflected the glory of God, and its brilliance was like that of a very precious jewel, like a jasper, clear as crystal. It had a very great, high wall with twelve gates. There were three gates on the east, three on the north, three on the south and three on the west. On the gates were written the names of the twelve tribes of Israel. Miles could then understand what God was foreshadowing in the Book of Numbers-2:1-34, *And the LORD spake unto Moses and unto Aaron, saying, Every man of the children of Israel shall pitch by his own standard, with the ensign of their father's house: far off about the tabernacle of the congregation shall they pitch.*

On the east side toward the rising of the sun shall they of the standard of the camp of Judah (the lion) pitch throughout their armies: and Nahshon the son of Amminadab shall be captain of the children of Judah. And his host, and those that were numbered of them, were threescore and fourteen thousand and six hundred. And those that do pitch next unto him shall be the tribe of Issachar: and Nethaneel the son of Zuar shall be captain of the children of Issachar. And his host, and those that were numbered thereof, were fifty and four thousand and four hundred. Then the tribe of Zebulun: and Eliab the son of Helon shall be captain of the children of Zebulun. And his host, and those that were numbered thereof, were fifty and seven thousand and four hundred. All that were numbered in the camp of Judah were an hundred thousand and fourscore thousand and six thousand and four hundred, throughout their armies. These shall first set forth.

On the south side shall be the standard of the camp of Reuben (the man) according to their armies: and the captain of the children of Reuben shall be Elizur the son of Shedeur. And his host, and those that were numbered thereof, were forty and six thousand and five hundred. And those which pitch by him shall be the tribe of Simeon: and the captain of the children of Simeon shall be Shelumiel the son of Zurishaddai. And his host, and those that were numbered of them, were fifty and nine thousand and three hundred. Then the tribe of Gad: and the captain of the sons of Gad shall be Eliasaph the son of Reuel. And his host, and those that were numbered of them, were forty and five thousand and six hundred and fifty. All that were numbered in the camp of Reuben were an hundred thousand and fifty and one thousand and four *hundred and fifty, throughout their armies. And they shall set forth in the second rank. Then the tabernacle of the congregation shall set forward with the camp of the Levites in the midst of the camp: as they encamp, so shall they set forward, every man in his place by their standards.*

On the west side shall be the standard of the camp of Ephraim (the calf) *according to their armies: and the captain of the sons of Ephraim shall be Elishama the son of Ammihud. And his host, and those that were numbered of them, were forty thousand and five hundred. And by him shall be the tribe of Manasseh: and the captain of the children of Manasseh shall be Gamaliel the son of Pedahzur. And his host, and those that were numbered of them, were thirty and two thousand and two hundred. Then the tribe of Benjamin: and the captain of the sons of Benjamin shall be Abidan the son of Gideoni. And his host, and those that were numbered of them, were thirty and five thousand and four hundred. All that were numbered of the camp of Ephraim were an hundred thousand and eight thousand and an hundred, throughout their armies. And they shall go forward in the third rank.*

The standard of the camp of Dan (the eagle) *shall be on the north side by their armies: and the captain of the children of Dan shall be Ahiezer the son of Ammishaddai. And his host, and those that were numbered of them, were threescore and two thousand and seven hundred. And those that encamp by him shall be the tribe of Asher: and the captain of the children of Asher shall be Pagiel the son of Ocran. And his host, and those that were numbered of them, were forty and one thousand and five hundred. Then the tribe of Naphtali: and the captain of the children of Naphtali shall be Ahira the son of Enan. And his host, and those that were numbered of them, were fifty and three thousand and four hundred. All they that were numbered in the camp of Dan were an hundred thou-*

sand and fifty and seven thousand and six hundred. They shall go hindmost with their standards. These are those which were numbered of the children of Israel by the house of their fathers: all those that were numbered of the camps throughout their hosts were six hundred thousand and three thousand and five hundred and fifty.

But the Levites were not numbered among the children of Israel; as the LORD commanded Moses. And the children of Israel did according to all that the LORD commanded Moses: so they pitched by their standards, (the lion, the man, the calf and the eagle) *and so they set forward, every one after their families, according to the house of their fathers.* Miles studied the layout of nations, and he could see a cross. He realized in the Scriptures from Genesis through Malachi of the Old Testament, God was using the Jews to point men to the cross of Christ.

Miles asked himself, "Why, in my lifetime, did I not realize there was something eternal in the making?" God had shown by His Word so plainly, in shadow, in type and pictures, these things he could now see in detail. He could not understand how he could have been so blinded. Jesus had said in John-5:39, *Search the scriptures; for in them ye think ye have eternal life: and they are they which testify of me.*

The wall of the city had twelve foundations, and on them were the names of the twelve apostles who established the Church. The City was laid out four square, as high as it was long and as wide as it was high. He realized it was approximately 1,400 miles long, 1,400 miles wide and 1,400 miles high. The walls around it were made of jasper, and the City was pure gold, as pure as glass. The foundations of the City walls were decorated with every kind of precious stone. The first foundation was jasper, the second sapphire, the third chalcedony, the fourth emerald, the fifth sardonyx, the sixth carnelian, the seventh chrysolite, the eighth beryl, the ninth topaz, the tenth chrysoprase, the eleventh jacinth, and the twelfth amethyst. The twelve gates were twelve pearls, each gate made of a single pearl. The great street of the City was of pure gold, like transparent glass. There was no temple in the City, because the Throne of the Lord God Almighty and of the Lord Jesus Christ was their one Throne. Again Miles saw other Thrones to the sides and in front of the Great Throne. He could see the sons of God on those Thrones, as they were the ones who had overcome. Again the Scripture came into his mind, Jesus had said, in-The Revelation-3:21,-*To him that overcometh will I grant to sit with me in my throne, even as I also overcame, and am set down with my Father in his throne.* He could understand these had not lived for themselves, they had overcome lust, greed, desire, passion, carnality and pleasure. They had been able after they were born again, to subdue the flesh with all the affections and lust thereof, and give themselves to the Lord and His service. Now and forever more they had their reward. Again the words of Jesus flashed across Mile's mind, Matthew 5:19-*Whosoever therefore shall break one of these least commandments, and shall teach men so, he shall be called the least in the kingdom of heaven: but whosoever shall do and teach them, the same shall be called great in the kingdom of heaven.* And also in The Revelation-22:18-19, *For I testify unto every man that heareth the words of the prophecy of this book, If any man shall add unto these things, God shall add unto him the plagues that are written in this book: And if any man shall take away from the words of the book of this prophecy, God shall take away his part out of the book of life, and out of the HOLY CITY, and from the things which are written in this book.*

The glory of God was the Light of the nations on

earth and they would walk day and night by that light forever and ever. That Light would also be for Miles in the Lake of Fire, day and night forever, but in the City was one endless, eternal day. Miles could see it was pure, and that the glory and honor of everything would be brought into it. Nothing impure could ever enter it. He could see the words of Jesus in The Revelation-22:14-15, *Blessed are they that do his commandments, that they may have right to the tree of life, and may enter in through the gates into the city. For without are dogs, and sorcerers, and whoremongers, and murderers, and idolaters, and whosoever loveth and maketh a lie.* Miles could understand the dedication to God on behalf of the people whom he had looked upon as weird; they were able to see all this before death, by faith. He could now see the faith of Abraham, and he could understand why he was called the Farther of so many in the faith. The Scripture that told of his faith stood out in He-brews-11:8-10, *By faith Abraham, when he was called to go out into a place which he should after receive for an inheritance, obeyed; and he went out, not knowing whith-er he went. By faith he sojourned in the land of promise, as in a strange country, dwelling in tabernacles with Isaac and Jacob, the heirs with him of the same promise. For he looked for a city which hath foundations, whose builder and maker is God.* It was plain to see, on that Mountain stood the everlasting foundation of all things. How clearly and definitely did he realize, that all things are and were created by God, and that they exist by His power alone. Miles cried out, "OH! great God, I know you are the God of all Gods and the Lord of all Lords, God please release me from this horrible place!" Deep down in his heart of hearts, Miles knew, God was God of His Word, and His Word said, Miles and the likes of him would go away into everlasting punishment, and that could not be changed.

He could see the pure river of the Water of Life, as clear as crystal, flowing from the throne of God down the middle of the great street of the City. On each side of the river stood the trees of life, bearing twelve crops of fruit, yielding its fruit every month. Oh! how Miles did yearn to go there and drink, or pick a piece of that fruit. It was such torment to be so thirsty, so hungry, and to be able to see, yet never allowed to touch.

There were shining golden mansions there, situated on either side of the streets that were pure gold, like transparent glass. The City was beautifully laid out and everything was in perfect order and balance. Peace, joy and eternal happiness were there, and could only be known by those who had the right to be there. Miles, in his mind could feel it at times, and OH! such sorrow, such sadness, such disappointment, everlasting anguish!

God's beauty of design was beyond comprehension; it was truly, the City of God. The trees of life were marvelous, standing by the pure sparkling River of Life. Miles cursed his existence, Why? . . . why? had he not believed the words that God sent into the world? He had spent his entire lifetime on things that really did not profit; things that were now burned up and existed no more. Now, to his sorrow, he realized the things of the Lord were the only things that were really important, the only things that would last. The knowledge and memory of the wasted opportunities and years, were all the more agony. He cursed the days he had spent on the earth as a man.

The promise where Jesus spoke of these things, flashed before Miles in John-14:2-3, *In my Father's house are many mansions: if it were not so, I would have told you. I go to prepare a place for you. And if I go and prepare a place for you, I will come again, and receive you unto myself; that where I am, there ye may be also.*

Miles knew this was the Heavenly Jerusalem, the exact center of everything and it would always be.

Suddenly Miles heard a very loud, wonderful voice from before the Throne saying, "Behold! . . . I make things new, *for the former things are passed away, and shall be remembered no more forever.*"

To Miles' sorrow, he knew that did not apply to him and all the others in the Lake of Fire. Miles knew his memory would remain the same. They of the Lake of Fire would remember and be troubled by that memory, day and night forever. But to his suprise, at the beginning of the first night after the change, he found a change was made for them in the Lake of Fire. The things out from the Lake of Fire were cut off at night and he could not see them, he was totally restricted to the Lake of Fire at night.

The next morning as Miles looked at the City, the Scripture flashed across his mind, in I Corinthians-2:9, *Eye hath not seen, nor ear heard, neither have entered into the heart of man, the things which God hath prepared for them that love him.'*

He watched the Sons of God, as they occupied their eternal, heavenly homes, they were so happy as they realized they were home at last, that was their place and it would always be. Miles could feel their joy, and to him it was awful, when he compared his with theirs.

Many of whom were forever free to go to the far reaches of eternity. Miles remembered how he used to sit out at night and look up into endless space and wonder what was really out there. Oh glorious liberty! Now eternity belonged to the sons of God; they had it all, they were the heirs of God, and joint-heirs with the Lord Jesus Christ. As heirs of God in eternity, they were infinite, having no boundaries or limits. The joy, the fulfillment and all that the eternal heart could desire, was theirs forever. They would never want nor need anything again forever. On the other hand, what deprivation, what eternal destruction! Miles was suffering! Oh!... Oh!.. the things that could have been. He wailed and he wailed, he cried and he cried, he rolled, jumped, hit himself, cursed, kicked and screamed, "Why? . . . Why? . . . Why? was I the way I was?" Ten thousand times ten thousand times, he asked himself this question.

He saw the earth was established out from the City and would orbit every 365 days. The earth had a spin of 24 hours, creating twelve hour days and twelve hour nights forever. It was beautiful and fruitful, beyond description! A mist went up at night and watered all things. There were no weeds, no insects, nothing to in anyway defile. It was pure; the Garden of Eden restored. The days were bright and clear, the temperature was perfect always the same. The nations of the saved on the new earth, were so full of joy, as they walked in the Light of the Glory of the City of God. The Kings and rulers would bring their gifts into the City of God and worship there before the Throne. They could see God's face and come into His presence. God's blessings and the peace that passes understanding was upon them always. There was no more death, nor sorrow, nor crying, nor pain, no more disappointments, no more failures, not even the shadow of turning. The knowledge of this Glory of the Lord was everywhere and it was beyond comprehension, and yet Miles could see it, and understand enough, that he knew he would long for it, and that would always be, forever, and ever and ever.—-OH! the eternal sadness.

THE CONSUMATION

20

The scope of what Miles was able to see and understand was limited to the Lake of Fire, the New Earth and the Holy City.

The things the Sons of God were able to do in eternity, outside that region of the macrocosm, Miles was not allowed to see. In his mind he could imagine some of the things they were able to do, but there was no way he could really know. But during the day he could see the ones within his scope. In fact it was as if he would be forced to zero in on each individual one at a time and feel what they felt, and see what they saw. There would be times when in his mind he would be with the redeemed souls on earth, and also in the Holy City. And then there were times when in his mind he would be with the damned in the Lake of Fire; what distress and anguish that was.

Miles could now fully understand the new creation. God had recreated all according to their works of a lifetime. The ones in glory were there because the blood of Christ covered their sin. The ones in the Lake of fire were there because their sins were open before God. The position each soul held in Glory, was according to his or her works, and the extent of the torment of each soul in the Lake of Fire was determined by his or her works. He realized God had picturized this by His creation on the earth and in the sea, which were only temporary. The Lord had created men and women for the earth, and no soul had control over where or how they landed on earth. In the creation of mankind through Adam, God had created some with white skin, some with black skin, others with brown, yellow and red skin. He had also created fish for the sea, some small and others great, in fact His power to create was without understanding and foolish men tried not to regard God by the teaching of evolution; the theory that groups of organisms change with the passage of time, mainly as a result of natural selection, so that descendants differ morphologically and physiologically from their ancestors. The historical development of a related group of organisms; phylogeny, a movement that is part of a set of ordered movements. But now Miles could see God had His reasons, known only to Him, for the things that came into being. He alone is Almighty God and He is bound only by His Word. The ones who accepted themselves as they were, and gave glory to God were happy, and had peace within. Therefore in the new Creation, each and everyone was set in his own lot. In reality they were what they chose to be. As for Miles, and all the billions in the Lake of Fire, their dreadful existence was without love, without music, without laughter, without fellowship, without joy. The horrible sounds of the groaning, cursing and crying was always a constant roar, so horrible. Miles knew he would never become fully adapted to this environment. His system would never fully build a resistance to his surroundings. He knew that the degree by which his physical system would adapt to this condition depended upon his works on earth. It was simple enough to understand, God had plainly stated in Galatians 6:7, *Be not deceived; God is not mocked: for whatsoever a man soweth, that shall he also reap.*

As the City would go out of sight across the western horizon, Miles would watch it. The night would set in, and that was worse than the day. The Lake of Fire gave off no light within itself, therefore the nights were very dark, lonely and full of pain. The night would shut off the things out beyond the Lake of Fire, and his concentration would be fully directed to his sad state there in the Lake of Fire. The time would drag oh! so slowly and he was all alone with the continual haunting sounds of the damned. He would yearn for the City to arise once again in the morning. Yet it was always distress and anguish to see the City, and a new day begin with no food nor drink. Such suffering, beyond words! He was so lost, so pitifully lost. But he had chosen that and he knew it, and had no one to blame but himself and the Devil. He knew that after ten billion times ten billion days and nights he would still be there looking and desiring, but nothing for him would ever change. He realized, and could see so clearly what it meant to be lost, without God , without hope forever. He would yell, he would moan and groan, he prayed, he cursed and screamed, but to no avail. The only effect it had, it annoyed the ones shut in also. They could hear each other, see each other, hate, despise and curse each other, but they could not communicate nor comfort one another. Each and everyone was alone in a place all his own. It was worse for Miles because he had been the supreme head, the man in charge of all the earth, now he was nothing, cast forever from the presence of God.

Oh! . . . he would be willing to do anything, if he could only go back. The way he had wasted his life with things that were now burned up, was an abomination to him. What a horrible predicament he was in. It was dreadful, yet that was the case; it was truly happening to him.

He had no control over his mind. For instance, there would be times when he could see men such as the Apostles. Paul was now a great King seated on one of the four Thrones before the Lord. Many, many billions of the redeemed gave glory to God on his behalf. He was among the Great in the Kingdom of God and his glory stood out like a shining star. His mansion was in the Holy City, next to Moses and Abraham. Miles was also forced to look at the old Prophets who were also among the Great ones, and seated on seats with the Lord. Miles wished he could blot these things out of his conscious mind, but no way would they go away. His mind was a constant reminder. This was confusion beyond understanding. Oh!——if only he could go back and stand once again in the fork of the road, as he had done moment by moment all the days of his life. He knew now beyond a shadow of doubt, one road had led to Heaven and eternal life, and the other had led to the Lake of Fire and eternal destruction. But there was no way; he would be as he was now, through out the eternities.

The most tormenting of all things to Miles though, was the open Bible, and the verses that kept coming into his mind, Isaiah-40:8 said, *The grass withereth, the flower fadeth: but the word of our God shall stand for ever.* This Word standing there before him, was a constant reminder of how spiritually blind and self centered he had been. God alone, whom he had refused to recognize, had the keys of death and hell, and he with the billions of others, would always see, and understand. Words flashed to haunt him in Proverbs-1:24-31, *Because I have called, and ye refused; I have stretched out my hand, and no man regarded; But ye have set at nought all my counsel, and would none of my reproof: I also will laugh at your calamity; I will mock when your fear cometh; When your fear cometh as desolation, and your destruction cometh as a whirlwind; when distress and anguish cometh upon you. Then shall they call upon me, but I will not answer; they shall seek me early, but they shall not find me: For that they hated knowledge, and did not choose the fear of the LORD: They would none of my counsel: they despised all my reproof. Therefore shall they eat of the fruit of their own way, and be filled with their own devices.'* He also saw, Romans-8:28, *For the wages of sin is death; but the gift of God is eternal life, through Jesus Christ our Lord.'*

In his lifetime there had been times when he would think on these things, but then they just did not make sense. The thought that a loving God would forever shut out a soul was an abhorrence to him, but now, here he was.

Miles could see the Devil and he cursed him for his deceitfulness. Why had he allowed him to rule his life? Why had he allowed that Spirit of disobedience to enter into him and possess him? The old liar! Miles hated him, but there was no way he could go to him. Ten million times ten million years and he would still have no less days. Oh! . . . if he could only get his hands on Satan.

Miles was now able to see and understand the over all plan of the Almighty, Everlasting Father. He knew, God, the Triune Godhead: God the Father, God the Son and God the Holy Spirit; for their own pleasure, had desired to create a generation of beings and sit them also into eternity. They created space and time and all the things that Miles could see and understand. This creation was full of light and very glorious. What was beyond in the endless eternity Miles would never know, it was just simply not for him to know. He realized no man can know anything unless God allows him to know. The Scriptures were there in his mind, 1 Corinthians-2:11, *For what man knoweth the things of a man, save the spirit of man which is in him? even so the things of God knoweth no man, but the Spirit of God.* And yet another, Deuteronomy 29:29, *The secret things be-*

long unto the LORD our God: but those things which are revealed belong unto us and to our children for ever.

Miles saw when God created a generation of beings and established over them a beautiful creature. He called Him Lucifer, which means the shining one, and he did shine above all others. Miles could see where Isaiah spoke of him in, Isaiah-14:12-16, *How art thou fallen from heaven, O Lucifer, son of the morning! how art thou cut down to the ground, which didst weaken the nations! For thou hast said in thine heart, I will ascend into heaven, I will exalt my throne above the stars of God: I will sit also upon the mount of the congregation, in the sides of the north: I will ascend above the heights of the clouds; I will be like the most High. Yet thou shalt be brought down to hell, to the sides of the pit. They that see thee shall narrowly look upon thee, and consider thee, saying, Is this the man that made the earth to tremble, that did shake kingdoms.* Miles knew what this prophecy taught. Lucifer coveted the very Throne of God. He was not satisfied with what he was given. That covetousness was sin, and God, Holy God, could not tolerate sin. As a result of Lucifer's action, God turned that creation inside out and darkness covered it all. The ones of Lucifer's kingdom were disembodied and became disembodied spirits, restrained in the darkness of eternity.

God the Son said, my Father, *"I will die to redeem the souls that are lost, will you accept my offering to cover their sin?"* This Christ said, with a heart full of love and compassion. His love for the ones Lucifer had taken down was beyond comprehension. Miles in his mind was there and he could not fathom the depth of the love of God the Son.

"Son, I'll give you a kingdom, and as the King of that Kingdom you will be an heir of God, and the ones you redeem will be joint heirs with you, do what you will," was

the decision of the Triune Godhead. Therefore, Christ stood as a Lamb slain before the world was.

God the son, said, *"Let there be light",* and there was light. He recreated the earth and created Adam and Eve. Then he implanted the first two disembodied spirits within them and they became living souls called man. Through them all souls moved into the realm of time, into the domain of mankind. In due time Christ the Son came into the world He had made. He passed through the womb of a virgin and grew up like an ordinary human being. He established his place upon the sand of time for 33 years The Apostle John wrote, in John-1:1-14, *In the beginning* (of things men are able to see and understand) *was the Word, and the Word was with God, and the Word was God. The same was in the beginning with God. All things were made by him; and without him was not any thing made that was made. In him was life; and the life was the light of men. And the light shineth in darkness; and the darkness comprehended it not.— He was in the world, and the world was made by him, and the world knew him not. He came unto his own, and his own received him not. But as many as received him, to them gave he power to become the sons of God, even to them that believe on his name: Which were born, not of blood, nor of the will of the flesh, nor of the will of man, but of God. And the Word was made flesh, and dwelt among us, (and we beheld his glory, the glory as of the only begotten of the Father,) full of grace and truth.*

Miles could see it all, and he could now understand it. He realized that in due time Jesus Christ died on a cross and shed His blood to defeat the power that Lucifer (Satan) held over all men. Almighty God had made a promise, He had said, *"When I see your blood I will pass over that soul."* Many many billions saw that great truth and plunged beneith that atoneing blood and were saved. Miles could see where Paul said in-Romans

5:8-9, *But God commendeth his love toward us, in that, while we were yet sinners, Christ died for us. Much more then, being now justified by his blood, we shall be saved from wrath through him.* Also he saw where Paul again said-Col 1:12-17, *Giving thanks unto the Father, which hath made us meet to be partakers of the inheritance of the saints in light: Who hath delivered us from the power of darkness, and hath translated us into the kingdom of his dear Son: In whom we have redemption through his blood, even the forgiveness of sins: Who is the image of the invisible God, the firstborn of every creature: For by him were all things created, that are in heaven, and that are in earth, visible and invisible, whether they be thrones, or dominions, or principalities, or powers: all things were created by him, and for him: And he is before all things, and by him all things consist.*

After the death of Jesus on the cross He ascended back to the right hand of God the Father and sent the Holy Spirit to empower and guide the Church. After the Church had fulfilled its purpose in time, Jesus called the Church unto himself and they of the redeemed stood before the Judgment Seat of Christ. That judgment was not a judgment for sin, it was a judgment of works, where every one received for the things done in his or her body according to their works on earth.

Miles could see the two old Prophets, they were two ordinary country preachers that God laid His hand upon. Neither if them had gained any greatness in life, they were unknown in the world of men, but they loved God and each had served him for the better part of fifty years. When the Rapture happened they were both caught up and transported by the power of God to Jerusalem. When they arrived, a man in the Jerusalem hotel, Mr. Vester said to them. "My grandfather who established this Hotel left a trust fund in 1910 with specific instructions. It reads, when the two Prophets ar-

rive from a far countery after the Rapture, this money is
for them."

The two Prophets were Brothers of the same father
but different mothers. In the late years of their lives
God reveiled to them in a dream what He was about to
do. He showed them the Scripture,-Numbers 12:6,
*And He said, Hear now my words: If there be a prophet
among you, I the LORD will make myself known unto
him in a vision, and will speak unto him in a dream.*
Miles could understand, that was the sign of a Prophet.

Their ministry was clearly foretold in the Scriptures
and Miles could see it, Revelation-11:3-13, *And I will
give power unto my two witnesses, and they shall prophesy
a thousand two hundred and threescore days, clothed in
sackcloth. These are the two olive trees, and the two candlesticks standing before the God of the earth. And if any
man will hurt them, fire proceedeth out of their mouth,
and devoureth their enemies: and if any man will hurt
them, he must in this manner be killed. These have power
to shut heaven, that it rain not in the days of their prophecy: and have power over waters to turn them to blood,
and to smite the earth with all plagues, as often as they
will. And when they shall have finished their testimony,
the beast that ascendeth out of the bottomless pit shall
make war against them, and shall overcome them, and
kill them. And their dead bodies shall lie in the street of
the great city, which spiritually is called Sodom and
Egypt, where also our Lord was crucified. And they of the
people and kindreds and tongues and nations shall see
their dead bodies three days and an half, and shall not
suffer their dead bodies to be put in graves. And they that
dwell upon the earth shall rejoice over them, and make
merry, and shall send gifts one to another; because these
two prophets tormented them that dwelt on the earth.
And after three days and an half the Spirit of life from
God entered into them, and they stood upon their feet;*

and great fear fell upon them which saw them. And they heard a great voice from heaven saying unto them, Come up hither. And they ascended up to heaven in a cloud; and their enemies beheld them. And the same hour was there a great earthquake. Miles knew that was the great earthquake that took place just after he had the two Prophets shot.

Now he could see and understand the Prophecy. He wondered why he did not see it before. He realized the Old Prophets had pointed it out to him when the Prophets were alive. He remembered the time he had turned the TV off and refused to listen. He realized that time was the unfolding of the Tribulation and the return of the Lord.

Miles could see it all so plainly, and he understood the plan that God had. He realized he had been blind to the plan and he would forever be on the outside looking in. God had given to Miles certain attributes like Himself. In spirit Miles was almost omniscient, to the point he was tormented beyond reason. To him it all seemed so unreasonable and unfair. He knew, God knew, before who would accept Christ and who would reject Him. He wondered, why did God bring the unbleivers into existence in the first place, did He get pleasure out of seeing them suffer? To Miles it just did not make sense. But then the words of God flashed before him, Isaiah 55:8-9, *For my thoughts are not your thoughts, neither are your ways my ways, saith the LORD. For as the heavens are higher than the earth, so are my ways higher than your ways, and my thoughts than your thoughts.* Miles realized although he did not understand God, he was in the Lake of Fire just as God said he would be. He wondered why he as a mere man had not taken the great omnipotent God at his word. God, alone was God and He would do whatsoever He wanted to do, and Miles hated Him for that. If only he had the power he would tear himself loose from the horrible place, but in his heart of hearts he knew it would never be.

The Words of the lowly Lord Jesus would always be there, in Mark-8:36-37, *For what shall it profit a man, if he shall gain the whole world, and lose his own soul? Or what shall a man give in exchange for his soul?*

Miles thought, OH! OH!—-if people could only see me now. I'm one soul that was alive on earth. I was alive, but I rejected the love of the God who made me.